Emily Harvale lives ii
– although she wou
French Alps ... or Canaua ... or anywnere that
has several months of snow. Emily loves
snow almost as much as she loves Christmas.

Having worked in the City (London) for
several years, Emily returned to her home
town of Hastings where she spends her days
writing ... and wondering if it will ever snow.

You can contact her via her website,
Facebook or Instagram.

There is also a Facebook group where
fans can chat with Emily about her books,
her writing day and life in general. Details
can be found on Emily's website.

Author contacts:
www.emilyharvale.com
www.twitter.com/emilyharvale
www.facebook.com/emilyharvalewriter
www.instagram.com/emilyharvale

***

Scan the code above to see all Emily's books on
Amazon

Also by this author

The Golf Widows' Club
Sailing Solo
Carole Singer's Christmas
Christmas Wishes
A Slippery Slope
The Perfect Christmas Plan
Be Mine
It Takes Two
Bells and Bows on Mistletoe Row

Lizzie Marshall series:
Highland Fling – book 1
Lizzie Marshall's Wedding – book 2

Goldebury Bay series:
Ninety Days of Summer – book 1
Ninety Steps to Summerhill – book 2
Ninety Days to Christmas – book 3

Hideaway Down series:
A Christmas Hideaway – book 1
Catch A Falling Star – book 2
Walking on Sunshine – book 3
Dancing in the Rain – book 4

Hall's Cross series
Deck the Halls – book 1
The Starlight Ball – book 2

Michaelmas Bay series
Christmas Secrets in Snowflake Cove – book 1
Blame it on the Moonlight – book 2

Lily Pond Lane series
The Cottage on Lily Pond Lane – four-part serial
Part One – New beginnings
Part Two – Summer secrets
Part Three – Autumn leaves

Part Four – Trick or treat
Christmas on Lily Pond Lane
Return to Lily Pond Lane
A Wedding on Lily Pond Lane
Secret Wishes and Summer Kisses on Lily Pond Lane

Wyntersleap series
Christmas at Wynter House – Book 1
New Beginnings at Wynter House – Book 2
A Wedding at Wynter House – Book 3
Love is in the Air – spin off

Merriment Bay series
Coming Home to Merriment Bay – Book 1
(four-part serial)
Part One – A Reunion
Part Two – Sparks Fly
Part Three ~ Christmas
Part Four – Starry Skies
Chasing Moonbeams in Merriment Bay – Book 2
Wedding Bells in Merriment Bay – Book 3

Seahorse Harbour series
Summer at my Sister's – book 1
Christmas at Aunt Elsie's – book 2
Just for Christmas – book 3
Tasty Treats at Seahorse Bites Café – book 4
Dreams and Schemes at The Seahorse Inn – book 5
Weddings and Reunions in Seahorse Harbour – book 6

Clementine Cove series
Christmas at Clementine Cove – book 1
Broken Hearts and Fresh Starts at Cove Café – book 2
Friendships Blossom in Clementine Cove – book 3

Norman Landing series
Saving Christmas – book 1
A not so secret Winter Wedding – book 2
Sunsets and surprises at Seascape Café-book 3
A Date at the end of The Pier – book 4

ISBN 978-1-909917-97-2

Published by Crescent Gate Publishing

Print edition published worldwide 2024
E-edition published worldwide 2024

Cover design by JR and Emily Harvale

Acknowledgements

My grateful thanks go to the following:

My webmaster, David Cleworth who does so much more than website stuff.
My cover design team, JR.
Luke Brabants. Luke is a talented artist and can be found at: www.lukebrabants.com
My wonderful friends for their friendship and love. You know I love you all.
All the fabulous members of my Readers' Club. You help and support me in so many ways and I am truly grateful for your ongoing friendship. I wouldn't be where I am today without you.
My Twitter and Facebook friends, and fans of my Facebook author page. It's great to chat with you. You help to keep me (relatively) sane!

For my dear friend, Rachel Taylor.
Thank you for the many years of friendship.
Friends since the age of five. Born just one
week apart. Still laughing after all these
years.

Emily Harvale

That Winter Night

CRESCENT GATE PUBLISHING

MAP KEY – BETANCOURT BAY

1) **Lookout Point** – At **310 feet**, this is the highest point on the white cliffs around Betancourt Bay. You can see Locke Isle from here while seated on the bench, and on a very clear day, even the coast of France. **Lookout Steps** lead down to the sandy beach – but there are **300 steps**, so most people access the beach farther along, where the cliff paths aren't so steep and there are fewer steps.

2) **Sunnycliff Cottage** - **James and Margaret Hart** live here. They have two daughters, **Fiona** and **Naomi**. Fiona lives in Folkestone with her boyfriend. Naomi is single and lives in Lewisham (London) where she rents a flat with two friends.

3) **Willow Cottage** – Home to **Malorie Blackwell**, a reflexologist.

4) **Seaview Cottage** – **Laurence Lake** lives here. He's a successful author of several cosy crime books.

5) **Rosehip Cottage** – **Jean and**

Victor Mills live here. Their four children, **Tom, Rob, Zoe and Tara** have all moved away but they come home for high days and holidays.

6) **Betancourt** – Ancestral home to the Betancourt family which currently consists of **Archie Betancourt**, his second wife, **Bianca** (his first wife **Francesca**, died) and his two sons, **Grifforde (known as Griff)** and **Russell.**

7) **Mr and Mrs Bernard and Barbra Brimble's B & B** – **Barbra** describes herself as 'a people person'; people describe her as 'a nosy gossip' – but not to her face. She loves to sing, and often does, whether others want her to or not.

8) **Clifftop Farm** – Once part of the Betancourt's estate, but now a small holding owned by **Sandy and Sonia Grey**, most of the farmland having been sold-off by various Betancourts over the years. Sandy and Sonia are known for taking in all sorts of waifs and strays, both human and animal.

9) **The Royal Oak** pub – Although highly unlikely, legend has it that King Richard (The Lionheart) once sat beneath the ancient oak tree opposite the pub, on his way to join the Crusades. Owned and run by **Freddie Tollard** and his daughter, **Charlotte (Charlie)**

10) **The White House** – Home to **Simon and Patience (Pat) Eversley** and daughters **Grace** and **Hope** along with their dog, **Lady Elizabeth, known as Lady E**. The Eversleys run an Events company, **Eversley Events** from here.

11) The Rectory – **The Reverend Brian Copeland** and his wife **Daisy** live here.

12) **St Gabriel's Church** – with a bijou village hall attached. The church was built in 1086, the hall in 1946.

13) **Catkin Cottage** – Home to **Hanna Shaw**, an artist.

14) **Acorn Cottage** – Elderly sisters, **Rita and Vera Boot** have lived here all their lives.

15) **Bluebell Cottage – Greg Bishop** lives here. He owns a bookshop in Folkestone.

16) **Oak View Cottage – Molly Law** has recently inherited this cottage from her grandmother, **Millicent**. Molly lives in Folkestone with her parents, **Owen and Nikki**.

17) **Betancourt Bay Café** – Owned by **Derek Dunpole** and his (miserable) wife, **Doris**, who had much grander plans than running a café in a small village, as she constantly reminds her long-suffering husband.

18) **West Wood** – owned by the Betancourts but they allow the villagers to use it.

19) **East Wood** – also owned by the Betancourts, who allow the villagers access.

Wish you were here?

This new series is set in Betancourt Bay, a fictional, clifftop village a mile from Folkestone. I've, sort of, 'demolished' everything that currently occupies this space in real life, and 'built' Betancourt Bay there instead. Apologies for that, but it was a necessary evil in order for me to tell these stories.

In addition to this, I have added a few fictional things/places/businesses in Folkestone – like the slipway where the Locke Isle Ferry docks, among others, so please forgive me for that!

This series also links to my other new series, Locke Isle, which is set on the fictional island of Locke Isle, two miles off the Kent coast, and also partly in the real town of Folkestone.

So if you know Folkestone and the surrounding area, you may not entirely recognise it when you read these books...

With love,
Emily xx

One

Boxed in on all sides and going nowhere, fast.

Hmm. How apt was that? *Going nowhere, fast.* That was the story of her life.

Naomi glared at the snaking rows of traffic all around her and almost laughed as Chris Rea bemoaned *The Road to Hell* via her car radio.

'I know how you feel,' she said, her knuckles turning white as she tightened her grip on the faded faux leather covering the steering wheel, which was closer to grey now than black. 'But you're singing about the wrong road. *This* road is the road to Hell.'

She huffed out a sigh and told herself to relax for the umpteenth time as she tapped her fingertips against the steering wheel in time to the music. The traffic was not moving and as there was nothing she could do to make it, there was no point in getting stressed about it.

But how could she relax? She was already nearly two hours later than she had planned, and it looked as if she might be stuck for another two.

At least it couldn't get any worse.

Could it?

Instinctively, she shot a look at the temperature gauge. The arrow on the dial had edged its way into the red and the little image that looked like an upside down key bobbing on water, had lit up. She stared in horror as it flashed at her.

'No! Don't you dare! Please. Not now. Not today.'

She tapped the glass cover in the vain hope that the arrow would drop back into the black, even though she knew it was a lost cause.

It wasn't the first time her battered old car had overheated but it was freezing outside right now. The roads and pavements still had snow and ice in several places from the blizzards during the first two weeks of January and although the last few days had been sunny and the snow was melting, it was cold enough for polar bears out there. Not that there were many of those wandering around the south east coast of England. But how could her engine overheat in arctic temperatures? Although she had been in this traffic jam for about an hour, moving at a snail's pace, and there had been two other jams before this one. Plus she'd been stationary for at least the last fifteen to twenty minutes with the engine ticking over.

Should she switch it off?

What if it wouldn't restart?

Judging by the expressions on the faces of the drivers and passengers in the vehicles surrounding hers, no one was happy, and they would all be even less so if they had to try to manoeuvre around her broken down car in the middle lane of the motorway. Better to keep the engine running and hope the traffic would start moving soon.

The most annoying part was, she could see the slip road she needed to take. She simply couldn't get to it.

She reached for her handbag on the passenger seat, and pulled out her phone, which was almost as ancient as her car. Fiona would be fuming, and so would everyone else, but this time they couldn't blame her. This traffic jam was not her fault. Although she should have called sooner. Why hadn't she done that? Too late to worry about that now.

'It's me,' she said, when her sister answered. 'And before you go mad, I'm almost there. I left in plenty of time but thanks to the icy roads and the miles of traffic, it's taking twice as long as it should.

I've been in this jam for an hour already and there were two more before this one. I should've phoned earlier, I know. I'm sorry. Why don't you go ahead without me and I'll meet you at the Bridal shop? No point in us all being late. Or possibly the restaurant, if this traffic jam doesn't move. ' She smiled apologetically even though her sister couldn't see her.

'Why am I not surprised?' Fiona said. She didn't sound as cross as Naomi had expected. 'Mum! You owe me a tenner. I told you she'd be late.'

'Excuse me!' Naomi snapped, miffed that her mum and sister had bet on whether she would arrive on time. 'I wouldn't have been if it hadn't been for this traffic. In fact, I would've been early.'

'And yet you're not, are you?' Fiona replied. 'You're late, as usual. Luckily for you, I'm in a good mood, so I'll forgive you. And I suppose we can rearrange your dress fitting. Where are you, exactly, and how long will you be?'

'I can see the slip road for home, but I'm boxed in and we're not moving even an inch, so I don't know how long I'll be. Once we start moving, about ten minutes or so. But as I said, I think it's best if I meet you in Folkestone. Either at the shop or at the restaurant.' She decided not to mention the temperature gauge or the red flashing light. 'I need to change.'

'That's something we can all agree on.' Fiona's voice was laced with sarcasm.

Naomi tutted. 'I meant, change my clothes.'

Yet even as she said it, she couldn't help but silently agree with her sister's retort. She did need to change. Or at least, her life did. Nothing seemed to go right for her, no matter how hard she tried. It was the complete opposite for her sister. Nothing ever went wrong for Fiona.

Not that Naomi begrudged Fiona's good fortune. She was pleased her younger sister's life was going exactly to plan. Fiona had the career she wanted, the flat she wanted, the boyfriend she wanted – now her fiancé after the marriage proposal she wanted – and the dream wedding she wanted was in three weeks' time. The three kids, two dogs, and the rabbit she had always said she wanted, would not be far away.

Naomi, on the other hand, had just been made redundant, finding a needle in a haystack might be easier than finding her own Mr Right ... or any man, for that matter, the flat she rented in Lewisham with two friends had been priced out of her reach – and theirs, by the notice of the rent increase that had been slipped through the letterbox

5

by their landlord two days before Christmas, and marriage, kids, and pets of any kind were but a distant dream.

And Fiona was right about her always being late. Even today, when she had promised their mum faithfully that she would be on time, and had left two hours early to surprise everyone, the universe or whatever had conspired against her and yet again, she was keeping everyone waiting.

'You'll be late for your own funeral,' Fiona had often joked. Now she said, 'We'll wait for another fifteen minutes. It'll be easier if we all go together. I'll call the shop and tell them we're running late, and I'll let Greg know we're behind schedule and may arrive at the restaurant a little later than expected.'

That wouldn't go down well.

The Bridal shop wouldn't be a problem; the owner was a friend of their mum's, and this was the final fitting for Fiona's wedding gown and for Naomi's bridesmaid dress, and, as they had both had a fitting when Naomi had been home for Christmas a little over three weeks ago, it was more of a formality than a necessity.

Greg on the other hand, would be cross. He was lovely, but he was a stickler for punctuality. Which was ironic really, bearing in mind he was a train driver – and the trains never ran on time.

Needless to say, he and Naomi did not exactly see eye to eye, mainly because she was always late. But also partly because one day, shortly after they had met, he had tapped his watch and raised his eyebrows at her, so she had pointed out that his obsession with time-keeping did not sit well with his chosen career path. Greg had not been amused.

Not that she would blame him if he got tetchy today. This was, after all, a special event. The first time both Fiona's family and his family were gathering en masse since the engagement had been announced six months before.

They had attempted to get the families together for this celebratory meal several times, but Greg's family was large. He had six siblings, most of whom had partners of their own and some of whom had kids, and both his parents also came from large families, which meant aunts and uncles and cousins, galore.

Half the problem was finding a restaurant with adequate seating and space to accommodate them all. The other half was that they all had busy lives. The third Saturday in January had been the one day most of them could make.

But who booked a restaurant for six p.m.

anyway? Okay, it was so that all the youngsters along with all the OAPs in his family, of whom there were rather a lot, could eat early and then be home in time for bed two hours later – both young and old, apparently – but really? The last time Naomi had eaten dinner at six in the evening was in her early teens.

'I really am sorry, Fi. I'll be there as soon as ... oh wait! We're moving! We're actually moving. Now I just have to get from the middle lane into the ... Hey! Don't honk your horn at me, you miserable sod. I'm indicating! Honestly. Some people shouldn't be allowed to drive. I'll see you in ten minutes, Fi. Bye.'

Naomi hung up, tossed the phone back into her handbag, and carefully edged her way from the middle lane into the exit lane for the slip road, accompanied by several more horns blasting, along with a few unsavoury hand signals, and a couple of near misses. But she was finally on her way again, so she really didn't care.

She couldn't wait to see her family. She hadn't seen them since Christmas, having spent New Year with her friends in London, and although she often went much longer than a few weeks between visits, for some reason she had been missing them more than usual.

It was probably because, ever since Fiona got engaged, all the talk was about the upcoming wedding, and living in London meant Naomi was missing out on much of the excitement involved with organising that. She and Fiona chatted frequently, as did she and her mum, but hearing all about it over the phone was not the same as being there.

But at least now she would be there for the final three weeks of preparations. Not that her family knew that yet. They thought she was merely coming home for the weekend, for the final fitting and the celebratory meal. They had no idea that she was hoping to be at home for a few weeks longer than that.

She had not told her family about the redundancy yet. It was not something she wanted to discuss over the phone and she didn't want to put a dampener on the wedding plans and the meal. And besides, even though she had known about it since the day after the New Year, the reality of it had not really sunk in.

Naomi had been told several months earlier that the building housing the Art Café of which she had been manager (and waitress when they were short-staffed) for the past three years, had been sold, but what she had not known was that the owners of the café, Benedita and John, having been unable to find suitable alternative premises in London, had made a snap decision that it was time to open a new café in Portugal. They had spent Christmas in Lisbon, where Benedita was originally from, and when they returned to England on January 2nd, they offered Naomi a job with them in the café they were buying. They seemed genuinely surprised when she had thanked them but said no.

'You often say you miss the sea,' Benedita had pointed out. 'Lisbon is the best of both worlds. A beautiful, vibrant city, and some of Portugal's best beaches only fifteen minutes away.'

Naomi had forced a smile. 'Thank you for the offer. But when I say I miss the sea, what I really mean is I miss Betancourt Bay, and my family. London is far enough away. Lisbon, sadly, is a stretch too far.'

'If you change your mind. You will always be welcome. And we will give you a redundancy payment of an additional three months. This has all happened so much faster than we expected,' Benedita had said with a shrug.

'You're not kidding,' Naomi had mumbled under her breath.

At least the redundancy payment would give her a few months to find a new job. As for finding a new place to live, that would require her actually having a new job, and as there was no sign of that, as yet, she had no alternative other than to ask her parents if she could return home. She could get a train to London to attend interviews, and once she had found a new position, she could commute for a time until she found a new flat. One of Naomi's flatmates was doing something similar by returning to her own parents and the other was moving in with her brother on a temporary basis. Naomi had met him, and she knew that particular arrangement would not last long. All three of them were hoping they would find another flat to share together but they all knew that might be easier said than done.

Now, she smiled at the sign for the sleepy, clifftop village that, despite having moved away many years earlier, she still thought of as home. Her parents, Margaret and James Hart, had lived there for most of their lives, having left Oxford where they had both been born and raised, because they wanted to begin their married life near the sea.

Betancourt Bay was where Naomi and Fiona had been born. Well, Folkestone General Hospital, to be precise, but Betancourt Bay was their home.

Their childhood had been idyllic. Long, summer days frolicking on the beach and

swimming in the sea, just a stone's throw –
and a steep path – from Sunnycliff Cottage.
Autumns spent foraging for conkers and pine
cones, and later in the season, for holly, ivy
and even mistletoe, in either West or East
Woods. Winters curled up on comfy sofas,
reading or drawing or knitting in front of the
wood burner in the cosy cottage, or baking
cakes and biscuits in the kitchen with their
mum. Although baking was something
Naomi had done throughout the year. She
was never happier than when she was in a
kitchen, baking. Spring had been Naomi's
favourite season, not only because it
heralded lighter nights and longer days, but
because it meant she and Fiona could dash
off to Clifftop Farm. She had always loved
that place.

Clifftop Farm had once been part of the
Betancourt Estate, but over the years, the
Betancourts had sold off chunks of it until
only a relatively small amount of land
remained. It was still a working farm when
Naomi and Fiona were young, and they had
helped the farmer, Mr Bean, and his wife,
feed the lambs, and the chicks, and the
piglets. But the Beans had both passed away
when Naomi was in her twenties and more of
the farm land had been sold off.

Now Clifftop Farm was just a small
holding with a few acres of land and was

owned by Sandy and Sonia Grey, but they had some sheep and other animals, and Naomi still popped round to feed the lambs, or for tea and a chat whenever she came back to Betancourt Bay.

Sandy and Sonia were known as good Samaritans by the rest of the village as they often took in all sorts of waifs and strays, both animal and human. Naomi never knew what or whom she might find in the Grey's cosy kitchen when she popped in for a cuppa.

The Betancourts had once owned all the land for miles around, but like the farm land, most of it had been sold off over the years. They still owned East and West Wood and various other parcels of land in Betancourt Bay, but they allowed the villagers free access throughout the year. They also opened their home and gardens several times each year as they hosted various events, from croquet, cricket, and tennis tournaments to picnics, parties and old-fashioned fayres in the grounds of Betancourt, their ancestral home. Most people's favourite was the Mistletoe Dance, held on Christmas Eve in the Grand Hall, but Naomi's was the Summer Fayre, held on both the front and back lawns. Although Betancourt was such a special place, everything held there was beautiful.

Naomi's bedroom overlooked the remaining grounds and gardens of the stately home, along with Lookout Point, an area of common land, once also owned by the Betancourts. When she was young, if she stood on tiptoe, she could see the top of the fountain in the Betancourt's back garden. She could also see the house itself, and both she and Fiona had often daydreamed of each marrying one of the Betancourt boys when they grew up. They had all played together when they were very young, along with the other children in the village, but both Grifforde (known as Griff) and Russell Betancourt had gone away to boarding school in their teens and everyone, sort of, grew apart and went their separate ways.

Naomi's best friend, growing up, was Grace Eversley, whose younger sister, Hope, was Fiona's best friend. Fiona and Hope were still close friends, but Naomi and Grace had drifted apart over the years. Naomi had gone to university but Grace had stayed at home in Betancourt Bay, despite having achieved perfect grades to attend almost any university she might have wanted to. Both Fiona and Hope had gone to university, although not the same one.

Naomi had moved to Lewisham on the outskirts of London when she was twenty-one, to share a rented flat with two friends she had met at university, and over the years she and Grace had seen less and less of one another. Fiona, on the other hand, like Hope, had returned home to Betancourt Bay after university. Hope had joined the Eversley family business. Fiona had worked in the human resources department of one of the largest insurance companies in the UK and had worked her way up to become the department head. She had recently moved into Folkestone to share a flat with her boyfriend, who had now become her fiancé.

Naomi and Grace still chatted like old friends whenever Naomi came home and they met up, sometimes for a coffee at either Grace's or Naomi's parents' cottages, or a glass of wine at The Royal Oak pub. But Grace was busy at the weekends, more often than not, because her family ran a hugely successful Events company, and that had grown even more successful over the fifteen years it had existed. The weekends were the only time Naomi was usually home, so finding time to see one another proved difficult, and as the years went by, they met up less often.

They had got together briefly between Christmas and Naomi returning to Lond for New Year, and Naomi had been astonished to discover that Grace had fallen in love with Griff Betancourt. She was even more amazed to discover that Griff had been in love with Grace for years.

'I thought it was Russell you had the hots for when we were growing up. And still did throughout your twenties if I remember correctly,' Naomi had said when Grace told her she and Griff were dating.

'Yes, well, the less said about that the better. You're right. I did think I was in love with Russell all those years. In fact I still thought it until fairly recently.'

'Really? What changed your mind?'

'Griff did. His family finally employed mine to organise the Mistletoe Dance this year and Griff and I had to spend quite a lot of time together. I thought I disliked him, but it turns out I didn't. I started having feelings for him, and when he kissed me under the mistletoe a few days before the dance. Phwoar! I realised I wasn't in love with Russell at all. I was in love with Griff. And although it's early days, I love him more and more each day. We spent the night together on Christmas Eve and I'm telling you, Naomi, I almost melted it was soooo hot!' Grace fanned herself with both hands to emphasize her point.

'Wow! I always thought there was something incredibly sexy about Griff. He had all that dark and broody stuff going for him. Russell was more angelic looking. But sexy in his way.'

'Hmm. Sadly my sister doesn't think so.

Me and Griff getting together wasn't the only thing that happened on Christmas Eve. Russell told me he loved Hope and had done for several years. He went off to tell her and ... let's just say, he didn't get his Christmas wish.'

'Oh no! Poor Russell. And how awkward for Hope.'

'It's awkward for everyone. Or it was. Hope made light of it saying that she knew he was joking and that he only said it because he had had too much to drink, and because Griff and I had got together. She was trying to let Russell down gently. Thankfully, he played along with it, but both Griff and I could tell he was heartbroken. I've been trying to remind her that he's a really good guy and that she could do far worse than give him a chance. But she says she doesn't want to get his hopes up only to have to let him down with a bang in the future. She's right, of course. But it would be so much nicer if she could fall in love with him.'

'If only life were that simple.'

'What about you, Naomi? Anyone you want to tell me about?' Grace had nudged her arm.

'Unfortunately, no. But if Russell is going begging, you could put in a good word for me.'

'Consider it done,' said Grace. 'Although

I can tell you that I know for a fact it's not a good idea to marry someone who is still in love with someone else. Let me tell you a secret. But promise me you won't tell anyone else.'

'Cross my heart,' Naomi had said. 'Oh. Not even Fiona? We tell each other everything. Or almost everything. But I won't tell her this if you say I mustn't.'

Grace pondered the matter for a second. 'I expect Hope will tell Fiona anyway, if she hasn't already, so yes. You can tell your sister.'

Naomi had listened in utter astonishment as Grace had told her the story about the relationship between Grace's mum, Pat Eversley, and Griff and Russell's dad, Archie Betancourt. When Grace had been called away shortly after, due to an emergency at one of the parties Eversley Events was organising, Naomi had raced into Folkestone and met Fiona for lunch.

And Folkestone was where both the Bridal shop and the restaurant they were going to this evening were situated.

If Naomi ever got there.

The road ahead was now traffic-free, but her car engine was making some rather worrying noises and the warning light seemed to be flashing faster now. Although that might simply be her imagination.

'Just a few more miles and we'll be at Mum and Dad's. Please don't give up on me now.'

A loud bang and a kind of spluttering sound was the response. And then, as Naomi managed to steer it to the side of the road, the car came to a slow halt and it hissed a final gasp.

Naomi resisted the urge to bash her forehead against the steering wheel and to scream and curse. Neither would make the car restart. The first might give her a headache and the second, a sore throat. Instead, she gripped the steering wheel tight and let out a silent scream.

That didn't really help either.

She reached into her handbag and with a lengthy sigh, pulled out her phone. It wasn't the end of the world. She could call home and ask either Fiona or their dad to come and get her. It would mean she'd have to leave her car where it was but she couldn't see any double yellow lines hidden beneath what was left of the days-old snow still covering the road and pavements in places, or any No Parking signs on the lamp posts, so it should be okay. She would have to call the breakdown service and let them know, but she'd have to meet them to get the car towed, and she couldn't do that tonight.

'No!'

Now she did scream. Her phone showed just one tiny signal bar – and then the screen went black as her battery died.

Two

It took Naomi a moment to work out exactly where she was. Having only recently left the motorway and taken the turn-off for Betancourt Bay, she was at the top end of London Road which meant she was about two miles from the 'Welcome to Betancourt Bay' village sign with its image of a seagull flying high above flower-strewn cliffs and an impossibly blue sea.

The nearest place where there would be a phone was Betancourt Bay Café, and that would be just over two miles away, if her calculations were correct.

It would take her approximately forty minutes to walk there. Thirty if she walked really fast, and maybe fifteen or so if she ran.

Running was not her strong point. She rarely even ran for a bus, so running two miles, especially on icy pavements and in the freezing cold, would be a challenge. She wasn't a couch potato, but neither was she what you would call, fit. Sport was something she occasionally watched on TV, not participated in.

And there was no way she could run in the boots she was wearing, especially as the roads and pavements were still so icy.

She raised her eyes skywards and yelled at the blanket of stars gradually popping up across the darkening sky.

'Why is this happening to me? It's not fair! Please give me a break. Send a car my way, pretty please. Or better yet, a dog walker with a phone. Anything or anyone. I don't care.'

But the stars merely twinkled at her.

At any other time she would be struck by the sheer beauty of the night sky, but this wasn't the time to appreciate the heavenly vista above her.

She simply had no choice. With a deep sigh, Naomi hauled the posh new holdall that Fiona had bought her for Christmas, from the back seat and placed it in the boot. There was no way she was going to carry that with her on this epic trek in search of a phone. Once she had called home, whoever came to pick her up could do a quick detour so that she could retrieve the holdall from her car. She was going to be so late now that another delay of a few minutes was not going to make much difference.

She closed the boot and locked it with the key. The car was too old to have the luxury of a remote, and the key-operated central locking it did have had died months earlier, so now each door, including the boot, had to be locked independently.

How she wished she could afford a new car. Or even a car a few years younger. This one might soon be considered vintage. Or more likely, scrap.

The car being scrapped wouldn't bother her, if she had the money to replace it. Some people loved their cars and even gave them names. Naomi had never done that. As far as she was concerned a car was simply a hunk of metal with wheels and an engine to get a person from A to B. Some of them were much better looking than others and some had hundreds of extra 'bells and whistles' but when it came right down to it, a car was a car. And right now, this car was pretty useless.

She grabbed her handbag, with her now also useless phone, from the passenger seat, threw the strap on her shoulder, and locked each of the car doors with the key. And then, with a determination worthy of a polar explorer, she set off towards Betancourt Bay.

Hopefully, she would meet someone along the way and they would be kind enough to let her use their phone. Assuming they had one with them. Then she could call home, and get the lift she desperately needed.

Or a vehicle would appear and she could flag it down. But although London Road was the main road into Betancourt Bay from the motorway and vice versa, hardly any vehicles travelled along it unless they were actually going to the village, or coming from it to the motorway. Everything else took one of the other roads, to Folkestone or to Dover, or north into the countryside.

And now that she had left her car far behind her, the road was rather creepy. She had never walked along it in the dark. Or in the daylight for that matter. There was nothing here but trees and bushes either side of the narrow pavements, and although there were street lights, the lamp posts were few and far between.

Perhaps she could run in her boots after all.

'Argghh!'

She tried to save herself but there was nothing to grab hold of and as she half-tripped, half-stumbled, she skidded on some ice and fell onto her knees. Fortunately, a large pile of snow left by the earlier blizzards and heaped at the side of the pavement broke her fall, but even so, she slid onto the wet pavement with a thud, sending aches and pains shooting through her entire body.

She wasn't sure what had happened at first, until she spotted that the heel of one of her boots had snapped and was hanging by a couple of threads of what appeared to be leather and rigid plastic.

'No!' she sobbed, dropping her head into her hands. 'These are my favourite boots.'

They were also the solitary pair of boots she owned. And the only footwear she had brought with her, save for her slippers and some strappy evening sandals, both pairs of which were in her holdall in the boot of the car. But as neither were suitable footwear for icy pavements and snowy roads, they could stay where they were.

Would the heel of her boot hold? She would have to limp and not put any weight on it but it was either that or break it off completely, and she didn't have the heart or the strength to do that. Leather and plastic were not the easiest materials to rip. She would need something sharp. Naomi didn't even have a pair of nail scissors.

Unlike Fiona, whose designer handbag contained a mini beauty parlour, including a manicure set with scissors, Naomi's faux leather handbag held merely the now dead phone, her half-empty purse with one maxed out credit card, a debit card for her overdrawn bank account, her Oyster card for the London transport system she would no longer be using (although thankfully, she had forgotten to top it up so the balance left on it was miniscule) and a few coins – no pound notes of any denomination. There was also a packet of tissues, a pair of sunglasses, a tampon in a plastic tube (it had been free with the pack and was rather pretty) a foldaway shopping bag as pristine today as it was when her mum had given it to her in a Christmas stocking several years ago, and a few old receipts for the bottles of wine and bags of salt and vinegar crisps she had sworn she would stop buying on her way home from her now former job, yet somehow still had. Nothing remotely useful for her current circumstance.

And what wouldn't she give for a bottle of wine and a bag of crisps at this precise moment?

Naomi left her handbag on the pavement as she struggled to get up, and was so engrossed in brushing off the icy clumps of discoloured snow that had clung to her coat, that she only spotted the cyclist when he was almost beside her. At least, she thought it was a 'he'. She couldn't really tell because the person was wearing black jeans, a large and baggy black hoody that covered most of the body as far down as the thighs, and a black scarf that hid the face almost entirely. The dark glasses over the eyes hid the rest of it.

'Oh! Thank God!' Naomi shrieked, grabbing her handbag from the pavement, and waving frantically, relieved beyond belief that someone had actually come along. Until she registered the fact that the cyclist was still peddling towards her at full pelt. 'Please stop. I need your help. Do you have a phone? Mine's dead and–'

For a mere second, she thought the person intended to run her down, but before Naomi had time to react, her arm was wrenched forward. She didn't realise her handbag had been taken until she saw the strap of her bag across the departing cyclist's body, the bike wobbling momentarily as he or she performed their criminal act and then raced away, sending Naomi tumbling onto the pile of snow for a second time.

Naomi's mouth dropped open in astonishment and all she managed to do was to point at the thief as she sat, bewildered on the snow. Not that she could have caught them even if she had reacted in a more productive manner. The person was already some distance away.

But had she really just been mugged? Things like this didn't happen in Betancourt Bay. In Folkestone, perhaps, but not here.

What should she do now?

What *could* she do now?

Could her life get any worse?

She had asked the universe for help; for it to send someone her way, and what had it done? It had sent her a mugger.

Distraught and helpless she glared up at the sky, as black as the clothes her mugger had been wearing, save for the myriad stars still twinkling down on her.

'Thank you very bloody much,' she hissed.

Her self-pity didn't last long and she soon got back on her feet, albeit somewhat shakily.

Now, in addition to calling home – and later, the breakdown service – she must call the police, her bank, and her credit card company. She needed to get to Betancourt Bay Café as quickly as possible.

And preferably before the universe sent someone else, this time to murder her, or something equally unpleasant.

She was sure there was a pathway somewhere along this road that led across the fields and onto Wood Lane and another path from Wood Lane to the café. She'd seen them hundreds of times over the years, but had never used either. Not that they would be visible beneath the layer of snow still blanketing the fields for as far as the eye could see. Which wasn't that far in the glow from the few lamp posts.

Did she need a path? A field was a field.

Just grass and earth below the snow. She had intended to cut across the fields farther on to get to the café in any event.

But now she wanted to get off this road as quickly as possible. The mugger might come back to see if she had anything else worth taking, like an expensive watch, or rings.

Was it good that she didn't have anything like that? Her sister did. But then Fiona's brand new, eye-wateringly expensive car would not have broken down. And if by some stroke of bad fortune it had, the battery in her brand new phone would not have died.

The only thing of value that Naomi had was the posh new holdall Fiona had bought her. Thank goodness she had left that in the boot.

Although … her car key was in her handbag. And her car was only about a mile up the road. The mugger was heading in that direction. Would he or she be bright enough to realise that the reason Naomi was walking along a dark and deserted road was because her car had broken down?

She was being silly. It might be dark but it was still early evening, so she could simply have been walking home from work, for all the mugger knew. Except her car was the only one on the road, and it was parked in the middle of nowhere.

There was no point in worrying about that now. She must get to the café and call for help.

She checked left and right for cars. Huh. As if! And then hurried across the road, as quickly as the broken heel of her boot would let her, to the pavement on the other side. From there she pushed through a gap in the low hedge and stepped onto the field.

Walking on snow covered frozen grass was slightly more difficult than walking on an icy pavement, oddly enough, but she moved as fast as she could with her broken heel.

The silhouettes of the trees of West Wood were visible in the distance, and as the wood bordered the top of Wood Lane, the café, which was a short walk from the lane, was not that far away.

It wasn't long before she spotted the warm glow that the lights of the café cast through the windows, and the beacon of hope gave her an added spurt of energy and determination.

She stepped over the low two-bar fence bordering the field and pavement of Wood Lane and her heart skipped a beat when she saw the A-frame sign on the pavement, pointing to Betancourt Bay Café.

She was about to cross the ancient cobbled road that formed Wood Lane when something on the pavement caught her eye and she glanced down. There, between the tiny islands and mounds of the residual snow, was a two pound coin.

Was the universe helping her at last?

She bent down and picked it up, smiling as if she had found a horde of treasure, not just one coin. But after the day – no, week – she had had, this *was* like finding treasure.

And she might need it.

If Derek was serving behind the counter this evening, he would willingly help her and would let her use his phone for free. If it was Doris, his wife, the coin would come in handy. Doris gave nothing to anyone for free.

Derek and Doris had a lease of the café, and had done for as long as Naomi could remember. It had been a long lease, as Doris was often complaining, but both Dunpoles had apparently thought it was a bargain at the time they had signed on the dotted lines.

Derek was okay, and even pleasant, if you caught him on a good day. Doris never had a good day. She was simply a miserable old … woman. And the years had made her more unpleasant, not less.

Few of the local residents ever went into the café these days, and so the only customers the café had were tourists, the occasional lorry driver who was lost, and the one friend Doris had – Barbra Brimble, owner of Brimble's B&B in the village. Both women believed they were destined for better things, but at least Barbra was pleasant ... to your face. She was known to gossip behind everyone's backs.

Doris, and her less than welcoming personality, was why the café was often empty during the winter months, and why it only opened now on Saturdays, and on Sunday mornings, out of season. During the summer it opened most days. Doris was known to complain even more in the summer.

Naomi opened the door of the café and sighed with relief, but it was short lived.

'We're closing in two minutes,' Doris said, without looking up from the magazine she was reading, as she sat on her chair behind the till, with a large cup in one hand. Derek was nowhere in sight.

'I just need to use a phone,' Naomi pleaded, stepping inside, and closing the door behind her. 'My car broke down on London Road and I've been mugged! A ... a cyclist stole my bag. And my phone was in it. But the battery was dead. I've had to walk across the fields, with a broken heel, and I'm absolutely frozen. I would die for a hot chocolate. I ... I've got this.'

She held out the coin she had found, her fingers shaking with cold despite the gloves she was wearing, but the warmth inside the café wafted over her and soon wrapped itself around her like a cloak.

Doris eyed her with contempt. 'If I had a pound for every time I've heard that story, I'd be living the high life in Spain. Which is where I would be if I hadn't married my good for nothing husband.'

'It's not a story! It's the truth!'

Doris sniffed dismissively. 'That won't buy you a hot chocolate. That won't even buy you a cup of tea. It'll buy you a Lottery ticket. Go and do that, and spin your unlikely tale to someone else.'

'What! Aren't you even going to let me use the phone?'

'No. I'm not. Now get out before I call the police.'

'Call them. I need to anyway to report my mugging.' Naomi held her ground, although she wasn't sure what was going on. 'You know me. I live here. Or I did. You must know who I am. My parents are ... Ooh. I feel...' A wave of exhaustion swept over her and she swayed as if she might pass out. And then everything went sort of misty.

Strong hands caught her and sat her on a chair. 'Hot chocolate, please,' a deep voice said. 'And a glass of water.'

'We're closing,' Doris snapped.

'You're open now. Unless you want a

seriously bad review, it would be wise to serve your customers. And quickly.'

'What's going on?'

Naomi recognised Derek's voice, but it was as if she were in the middle of a heavy sea mist and couldn't see clearly. She could just see shapes of people and the voices sounded far away.

'This woman needs water,' the deep voice said. 'And a hot chocolate. Your wife ... or colleague, or whatever has refused to help.'

'Oh goodness! I'll get some water.' There was a scuffling sound followed by Derek adding, 'Here. Take this.'

'Can you hear me?' The stranger's voice held genuine concern. 'Drink this.'

A bottle of water touched Naomi's lips and she drank from it.

'Should I get something stronger?' Derek asked, sounding worried. 'Like brandy?'

'I don't like brandy,' Naomi said between gulps as she tried to sit upright. 'But I would like a hot chocolate. Please.'

'Oh yes. Coming right up,' said Derek.

'I'm not making her hot chocolate,' Doris hissed.

'I didn't ask you to,' Derek said. 'I'll do it.'

'Well someone needs to pay for it. This isn't a charity. And she's putting on an act.'

'I'll pay for it,' said the deep voice. 'And this is no act.'

The water helped; but it was the hot chocolate that did the trick. Naomi finally managed to focus. And when she did, she nearly choked with surprise.

She was staring into the most spectacular eyes she had ever seen. A sort of blue-grey with added sparkle. The stunning eyes were encased by long, brown lashes, above which sat straight brows with a small furrow between them hinting at the owner's concern. Tiny creases fanned out into a tanned face with a nose that had probably once been perfect, and even though it had clearly been broken at some stage, was still rather nice. Beneath that sat a mouth that was made for kissing, set above a firm jaw with a shadow of stubble. His hair was thick and short on both sides but an off-centre parting gave way to a slightly longer wave of lustrous brown, a few strands of which fell across his forehead.

'Oh!' Naomi said, surreptitiously taking in the rest of him. He was sitting on a chair beside her so she couldn't tell how tall he was but judging by the broad shoulders and solid looking torso hidden only by a polo shirt and jumper that seemed to want to cling to him (and who could blame them? She wouldn't mind clinging to him herself) plus the angle of his legs, which appeared to be long and muscular beneath his jeans, he was fairly tall.

'Hello,' he replied, in that smooth, deep voice. 'Are you okay? I think you may have passed out for a second. Do you know where you are? You said you'd been mugged. Are you hurt? You look a little … bewildered, if you'll forgive me for saying so.'

Naomi suspected she would be willing to forgive him anything. Well almost anything. Some things were unforgivable. Like mugging unsuspecting women. Or cheating on a partner. Or moving to Portugal and leaving your employees in the lurch.

No. That was unfair. And none of those things had anything to do with this handsome stranger.

'Erm … I don't think so. No. He – or she – just took my handbag. And yes. I know where I am. I … Oh! Do you have a phone I could borrow, please?'

'To call the police? Yes of course.'

'No. To call my sister.'

Three

'If you're trying to sell me something, forget it,' Fiona said, clearly assuming this was a cold-call from a phone number she did not recognise, and she promptly disconnected the call, having already declined Naomi's two earlier attempts. In frustration, Naomi sent her a text saying:

'It's Naomi. I'm trying to call you from an unknown number. Not a scam. Please answer!'

This time when Naomi called, Fiona simply said, 'Hello?' But the doubt in her voice was apparent.

'Fi! It's me. Don't hang up. And don't be cross. I've been mugged. And my car has broken down. I'll explain later but I'm in Betancourt Bay Café and I really need someone to come and get me.'

'Wh-what! Is this some kind of joke? How do I know it's really you?'

'It's no joke, believe me. I'm serious. And

of course it's me. Surely you recognise my voice?'

'Y-eah. But you could be someone using one of those computer generated voices.'

Naomi tutted loudly. 'Don't be ridiculous. It's me. I'm late for the dress fitting and the party. But then again, I'm always late. Does that prove it's me?'

'Naomi? What's going on?'

'I just told you. I've been mugged. I would've walked home but I've broken a heel and just getting here was a struggle. I know how important this evening is to you and Greg, and to Mum and Dad, and I'm sorry. But I really do need help. Can you ask one of them to come and pick me up, please? My handbag was stolen. And my phone, although that had ... never mind. I'm calling from a good Samaritan's phone. Erm ... Fi? Fiona? Are you still there?'

'Yes, I'm here. I'm just trying to take this in. And Greg's asking who I'm talking to. Were you really mugged?'

'Yes. Do you honestly think I'd make that up?'

'No. Of course you wouldn't. Are you hurt?'

'A little bruised. But that's because I fell. I sort of fainted a bit just now and I'm feeling a little weird, but I think I'm okay.'

'Oh my God! Where did you say you

were?'

'Betancourt Bay Café.'

'And the Dunpoles have been good Samaritans? Really?'

'No. Someone else has. Can we discuss this later, please?'

'Yes. Yes of course. We're coming. Stay there.'

'I intend to. Thanks, Fi.'

The handsome stranger had moved away to give Naomi space and privacy to make her call but now he smiled at her.

'Is someone coming for you?'

'Yes. One of my parents. Thank you for letting me make that call. My sister didn't recognise the number. Obviously. Which is why it was a while before I spoke to her. I had to send her a text to tell her it was me.'

'No problem.'

'Well,' said Doris, glaring at her. 'You'll have to wait outside. We should've closed ten minutes ago.'

'Don't be so ridiculous, Doris!' It seemed Derek Dunpole had decided that it was time he stood up to his wife and said what he thought. 'She can wait in here. It's freezing outside. And the woman has just been mugged.'

'Then why did she call her sister and not the police, eh? Answer me that.'

'Erm. I'm going to call the police,' Naomi

said. And then to the handsome stranger. 'May I make another call, please?'

'Of course.' He smiled warmly at her before glowering at Doris.

Naomi dialled 999 and explained what had happened. The female call centre operator asked several questions and Naomi answered as best as she could, but her head started throbbing, and when the woman asked if the perpetrator had used violence or intimidation, she wasn't sure what to say.

'Erm. I fell to the ground, but I can't remember if the person pushed me, or pulled me over when they grabbed my bag.'

'Are you hurt?'

'Erm. Bruised. And apparently I sort of passed out just now,' she said, repeating what she had told her sister. 'But I'm fine. I think. I'd already fallen over before I was mugged.'

'Have you been drinking this evening?'

'No! I was driving down from London and my car broke down, which is why I was walking. But I broke my heel and fell. I got up and then the cyclist stole my handbag, with my purse, car keys, and mobile phone inside.'

'Are you still at the scene?'

'No. I had to walk to Betancourt Bay Café to borrow a phone.'

Naomi was beginning to wish she hadn't made this particular phone call, but after a few more questions, the operator seemed to have all the information she needed.

Doris looked on, her confident and contemptuous expression faltering slightly as Naomi rang off and returned the phone to its owner.

'They're sending an IRV and officers will come and take my statement,' Naomi said. 'I didn't know what that was but the operator told me it's a patrol car and that it happens to be nearby. She asked me to sit tight. Although not in those words.'

'It's an incident response vehicle,' the stranger said. 'So yeah. Basically a patrol car. Although I think some IRVs are fitted with specialist equipment for certain incidents. That's not important.' His smile made Naomi feel as though everything would be right with the world.

'See!' snapped Derek, grabbing a straw broom that had been leaning against the counter, with one hand and wagging a finger at his wife with the other. 'The poor girl has been mugged. And you didn't believe her.'

'I don't want the police coming here!' Doris shrieked.

'Why not?' Derek asked, as all eyes turned to her. 'We don't have anything to hide. And it's a good thing they're treating it as a priority. We don't want criminals running around Betancourt Bay. Business is bad enough now. No one will come here if they think they might be attacked nearby. This has always been such a safe village. I think this is the first crime I've heard of since we moved here, more years ago than I care to remember.'

'I think you're right,' Naomi said. 'Oh. I forgot to tell her someone's coming to pick me up. Perhaps I should've waited and phoned from home. Although aren't you supposed to report a crime as soon as possible?'

'That's what you should've done,' Doris said. 'Or gone directly to the police station. This has nothing to do with us and we shouldn't be dragged into it.'

'I ... I'm sorry,' Naomi said.

'You won't be dragged into anything,' said the stranger, narrowing his eyes at Doris. 'And treating people kindly should be something you should want to do. Has no one ever told you that?'

'Why are you still here?' Doris growled.

And then all hell broke loose.

'Leave the young man alone, Doris.' Derek's face was red but his knuckles were white where he was clenching the broom handle so tightly. 'He's right. A little kindness goes a long way.'

'I wish you'd go a long way,' grumbled Doris, loudly.

'And I wish you would too!' Derek roared.

'Don't you raise your voice to me, Derek Dunpole! I should've listened to my mother. She told me you'd never amount to anything.'

'I should've listened to mine. She told me there was something unpleasant about you.'

'Your mother was nothing but a silly old bag. And she molly-coddled you and turned you into a wimp of a man.'

'That's it!' Derek banged the broom on the floor but it had little impact as it was made of straw. 'I've had enough. This is the final straw. You can bloody well go to Spain, Doris. And the sooner the better. We'll sell what's left of the lease, which won't fetch much as there's not long left, and then I want a divorce.'

'What!' Doris gasped, looking as if she had been slapped across the face. 'Well I won't give you one. So there. You'd be nothing without me. Nothing.'

'I'll be happy without you. And that's everything.'

'Derek! You don't mean that. You can't,' Doris pleaded.

'I can and I do.'

She narrowed her eyes at him. 'I'll take you to the cleaners if you try.'

'I'll take you to Lookout Point and throw you over the edge if you do.'

Doris shrieked, although she didn't look particularly concerned. 'You're threatening to kill me? I'd like to see you try.'

'I should've done it years ago. Or jumped myself.'

'Jump? You? Don't make me laugh. I'd have to push you. You never do anything unless I make you.'

Naomi sat bewildered and watched the couple arguing. For people in their sixties, they were behaving a lot like children. She knew from local gossip that this was not their first row, but she had been told that Derek had borne the brunt of Doris' vitriol during previous confrontations. This evening he appeared to be intent on giving as good as he got.

The handsome stranger sat beside Naomi, perched on the edge of his seat, as if he thought she might need protection. He glanced at her, his brows furrowed, but neither he or Naomi spoke.

'You're nothing but a bully. A big, fat, ugly, bully,' Derek yelled.

'I am not fat. Or ugly. How dare you! I could've had my pick of men, you know. You weren't the only one who asked me out.'

'I was the only one stupid enough to ask you to marry me!'

'I was the one who was stupid. I should've left you at the altar and run off to

Spain.'

'Oh how I wish you had!'

The handsome stranger stood up. 'Erm. Look. This is none of my business but–'

'No! It's not,' hissed Doris.

'Stay out of this,' advised Derek. 'For your own good.'

'Was that a threat?' said the stranger, with a hint of a sardonic laugh. 'Because I don't think–'

'Shut up!' Doris and Derek bellowed in unison.

The man seemed torn as he shot a look at Naomi, who nodded.

'I think you should leave them to it,' she said.

'But the way this is going, one of them might do something foolish.'

'The police should be here soon, remember. Best to let them handle it.'

He hesitated for a moment and then sat down but he looked ready to pounce if the situation got out of hand.

In the midst of the argument, Naomi's sister, Mum, and Dad turned up. They had all clearly jumped in the car and raced from the restaurant in Folkestone to the café in Betancourt Bay, a mere few minutes' drive away.

'I've left Greg with his family because I had to come and see for myself that you were really okay,' Fiona said, stopping in her tracks in the doorway. 'What on earth is going on here?'

'I'm fine. I think. It's those two I'm worried about,' said Naomi, as the stranger stood up again. 'They're having a humdinger of a row.'

'We can see that, sweetheart,' said James, squeezing past his other daughter and giving the stranger an odd look.

'I wondered when this would happen,' said Margaret. 'Time to go, I think. Best leave them to it, darling.'

'I've called the police,' Naomi said, still seated. 'For me. Not for them. Although...'

Doris and Derek's voices had grown louder and neither of them appeared to have noticed the arrival of Naomi's family. Doris threw a coffee cup at Derek, which narrowly missed his head, and smashed against the wall behind him. He batted the second one away with the straw broom, and that landed on the floor just a few feet from Naomi's chair.

Now, everyone was yelling. Or almost everyone. The stranger sounded surprisingly calm and collected as he asked Doris to stop throwing things, and told Derek not to do anything he might regret. James joined him, but seemed unsure of what to do as Doris appeared to be searching for more ammunition.

'The only thing I regret is marrying her!' Boomed Derek.

'I hate you!' Doris screamed.

At that moment two police officers burst through the door. They had obviously been told by the call centre that they were attending to take a statement from a mugging victim, but they had clearly heard the shouting and screaming and instead found themselves breaking up a domestic dispute, with a wife now wielding a coffee pot and a husband wielding a raised broom.

The stranger had been trying to intervene, but was pushed aside by one of the officers, and James was pulled away by Margaret just as he was about to grab Doris.

At one point in all the commotion, the police officers threatened to arrest everyone for affray. Luckily, once Doris and Derek had eventually been silenced, Naomi and the stranger were able to explain what had happened.

One of the police officers then told the Hart family to go home, saying fellow officers would call round later to take Naomi's statement, both in connection with her mugging and also with the events in the café. The other officer must have been saying something similar to the stranger, Naomi assumed, but as Derek and Doris started arguing again, the officer closest to the Harts hastily ushered the family out of the café, and so Naomi didn't know what happened next, or where the stranger went after that.

More than a little bemused as they got into Fiona's car, Naomi told Fiona and their parents to go back to the restaurant.

'If you could just drop me home, that would be great. If I'm feeling up to it, I can join you later after the police have been and gone. But can we make a quick detour to London Road first, please? I left my holdall in the boot.'

'Of course,' said James, even though it was Fiona who was driving. 'Best not to leave anything of value in there, just in case. I'll call the breakdown service once we get home. They'll soon get your car sorted out.'

'I wouldn't bank on that,' said Naomi. 'I think it might've taken its final gasp.'

'Let's wait and see what they say,' said James.

'If you think we're leaving you on your own after the day you've had, you can think again, young lady,' said Margaret, sounding every inch the former school headmistress that she had once been.

'Mum's right. We're staying,' said Fiona. 'I'll call Greg and tell him. He'll understand.'

'No. Please don't do that, Fi. I've already ruined your day more than enough. You go and have fun.'

'Just how much fun do you think I'll have knowing that you're sitting at home being grilled by the police? We can rearrange the celebration. We've already rescheduled the Bridesmaid's dress fitting.'

They were hardly the same thing, but Naomi didn't bother to point that out.

No matter how many times she assured them all that she would be fine left on her own, they simply wouldn't budge. In truth, she was glad of that. She was still a little shaken up and being left alone was actually the last thing she wanted.

What she did want was a relaxing and soothing bath. And a glass of wine. And possibly a bag of salt and vinegar crisps.

It only took a couple of minutes to reach her abandoned car, and Fiona pulled up right in front of it.

'Have you got the key?' James was sitting in the passenger seat beside Fiona and he twisted round and held out his hand.

'The key?' Naomi repeated, glancing from him to her mum and then to Fiona. 'Erm. It was in my handbag.'

Everyone looked at her with raised eyebrows.

'Never mind,' said Fiona. 'Leave this to me. Pass me my handbag, please, Dad.'

It was in the passenger footwell and he

reached down to retrieve it. Fiona took it from him and a second later, pulled out what looked like a manicure set. It would have taken Naomi a lot longer than a second to find anything in her own handbag, despite the fact that it was virtually empty, but then Fiona had always been well organised.

'What are those?' Naomi asked, when Fiona flipped it open revealing a row of odd looking little keys and screwdrivers inside.

'Greg bought it for me,' Fiona said. 'And one of our friends showed me how to pick a lock.'

'I don't think I want to hear that,' said Margaret, as Fiona shoved her car door open and got out.

'Best not mention this to the police,' said James, doing likewise.

Margaret and Naomi exchanged glances on the rear seat before following Fiona and James to the boot of Naomi's car.

Luckily it didn't look as if the mugger had put two and two together. The boot was still locked, as were all the doors. Fiona had checked each one just in case. She removed two of the long keys and stuck them in the lock on the boot.

'Are you sure you can ... Oh! You've done it.' Naomi wasn't sure whether to be pleased or concerned.

'That's a really rubbish lock,' said Fiona,

pulling a face at her.

'It's a very old car,' replied Naomi, thrilled to see the holdall was in the boot, exactly where she had left it.

James reached in and grabbed it, slamming the boot shut.

'I think I might be able to lock it again,' Fiona said. And a second later, she smiled. 'Done. Let's get home.'

'Yes,' said Margaret. 'Before we all get arrested. Or freeze to death. It's really cold now.'

'It's been really cold all day,' Naomi said, linking her arm through her mum's. 'I wonder if that's why I sort of fainted. Perhaps I had a touch of hypothermia after trudging across the fields.'

'I suspect it was the shock that did it,' said James.

'Delayed shock?' Naomi nodded. 'You're probably right, Dad.'

'Maybe we should take you to the hospital, just in case,' said Margaret, reaching across to touch Naomi's forehead.

'No thanks, Mum. I've had enough excitement for one day. I just want to go home and soak in a long, hot bath.'

'What about a short, hot bath?' joked Fiona. 'Blimey. Mum's right. It really is cold, isn't it?'

They hurried back to Fiona's car and a

matter of minutes later, they all rushed into Sunnycliff Cottage.

They threw off their coats, boots and shoes in the hall and dashed into the sitting room, plonking themselves in front of the wood burner as James tossed more logs onto the banked-up fire. It only took a minute or two for the flames to burst back into life.

Once they were all warm again, Margaret drew Naomi a bath and added some of the expensive bath oils that Fiona had bought her for Christmas.

'That smells so good, Mum. Thanks,' Naomi said, and felt better just breathing in the scent of English Pear and Freesia.

As she luxuriated in the wonderfully warm water, she wondered where the handsome stranger was. Would he be taking a soothing bath somewhere? Was he telling his girlfriend or wife about the strange events of the evening? Was he somewhere in Betancourt Bay? Or was he driving to his home, which might be miles and miles away from here?

Why hadn't she asked him for his name? Or his phone number.

Probably because she had been in a state of shock, as her dad had suggested. It's not every day that you get mugged. Especially in a place like Betancourt Bay.

Nevertheless, she was cross with herself.

Would she be able to find out who he was? Would she ever see him again?

The thought of not seeing him again made her even more cross, so she tried to put all thoughts of him from her mind.

She put on a pair of PJs and over those, her fleecy dressing gown, slid her bare feet into her slippers, and went back downstairs to rejoin her family.

'Did any of you hear the other man in the café say his name?' Naomi asked, settling herself beside Fiona on the comfy sofa in front of the now roaring fire, as James handed her a large glass of Bailey's. They all had a glass of that in their hands.

'Not me,' said Fiona. 'Why?'

'Because he took really good care of me and I'd like to thank him. He let me use his phone. He bought me a hot chocolate. And he waited with me for you to arrive. Of course I didn't know you would all be arriving, but anyway.' She rolled her eyes at them and smiled. 'I'm glad you did. It's just that I'd like to repay him for his kindness.'

'I didn't hear him say his name,' said James.

'Nor me,' Margaret added.

'Perhaps the police will know,' Fiona suggested.

'Maybe. Should you be drinking Bailey's when the police are coming? Bearing in mind you've got to drive back to Folkestone tonight?' Naomi said.

Fiona tutted. 'You know I don't drink and drive. Greg offered to come and get me, but I told him I wanted to stay here tonight.'

'Why?' Naomi asked. 'Not because of me, I hope.'

'No. Because of me. I want to be sure my sister is really okay.'

Naomi beamed at Fiona. 'I'm fine. Honestly. But thank you. It'll be lovely to have you staying here, just like the old days.'

'Not so much of the old,' laughed Fiona.

When the police officers arrived to take Naomi's statement about an hour later, she did ask them who the man was who had helped her, and how she could get in touch with him, but they told her they could not give out such information.

'I just want to thank him for letting me use his phone. And for buying me a hot chocolate,' she said. Repeating what she had told her family.

'We'll pass on your thanks,' one of the officers said. But would say no more than that.

Naomi did not know if they would, or not, but she had no choice other than to leave it at that.

She would have to find another way of getting in touch with her handsome stranger.

Not that he was 'hers', of course.

But something inside her told her that she would very much like him to be.

Four

Naomi's entire body ached by the time she went to bed and although the wonderfully soothing bath had helped relax her tense and aching muscles, as had the two or three glasses of Baileys, she felt as if she had been used as a ball and kicked around a football pitch.

She had intended to stay up late and chat with Fiona but the heat of the fire and the fact that it had been a long and somewhat eventful day, meant she could not stop her eyes from closing and by ten-fifteen p.m. she was tucked up in the double bed in the pale blue and soft lemon-yellow room she loved so much.

Many people had fond memories of their childhood bedrooms but Naomi's bedroom had always felt like a sanctuary to her. Not that she had needed a sanctuary that often. Her childhood had been idyllic, her parents loving, understanding, people, but like everyone, Naomi had shed a few tears over angry words spoken, friendships lost, teenage hearts broken by boys who had not deserved her young love, and beloved pets that had passed over the rainbow bridge.

Even as an adult she breathed a contented sigh the moment she stepped inside, and the sigh she had breathed tonight was more pronounced than usual. She had cursed the universe for her redundancy, the rent increase, the traffic jams, her car breaking down, her broken heel, and the mugger coming her way. Shc had forgotten, until she opened her bedroom door, that she had three month's pay, a loving and welcoming home to go to where food would always be on the table and a warm and comfy bed awaited, and that people loved her. She was luckier than many.

'Glad to be home?' Fiona had asked, following her inside.

'More than you can imagine,' she had replied.

And as she snuggled down beneath the winter duvet while the bare branches of a tree shaken by the bitterly cold January winds rapped against her window, there was nowhere else she would rather be.

Fiona sat on the edge of the bed for a few minutes but could obviously see how tired her sister was.

'I'll let you get some sleep and we'll chat in the morning. Yell if you need anything in the night. I'm only next door.'

'Good night, Fi. And thanks for everything.'

Naomi knew her sister meant well but a nuclear explosion wouldn't wake Fiona. Luckily, their parents were light sleepers. Naomi didn't think she'd get much sleep, even in her comfy bed, but she would try not to trouble them. She might be a bit battered and bruised but she wasn't exactly helpless. If she wanted anything in the night, she was perfectly capable of getting it herself.

She was surprised when her mum opened the curtains and bright sunshine shone through the glass panes like a spotlight on Naomi's face. She opened her eyes and quickly closed them again.

'What time is it?' she asked feeling far less achy and sore than she expected.

'It's almost nine, sleepy head,' said Margaret.

'What? Why didn't you wake me sooner?'

'You were dead to the world. You clearly needed to sleep. But I knew you wouldn't want to miss breakfast. It's later than usual because we all overslept. Your dad and I didn't get up till eight and you know we're usually early risers.'

'I'm starving,' said Naomi. 'Do you mind if I eat first and shower after?'

Margaret laughed. 'Of course not. Fiona's doing the same. She overslept too. How are you feeling this morning?'

'Not as bad as I thought I might. I thought I'd be stiff and bruised this morning but I hardly ache at all.'

'It's those magical bath oils,' said Margaret.

'Or the magical Bailey's,' Naomi laughed, throwing off the duvet and getting out of bed.

She stretched her body out before wrapping her dressing gown around her, although the bedroom was as warm as toast, and slid her feet into her slippers. Then she and Margaret went downstairs to the kitchen where James and Fiona, both still in PJs and dressing gowns, were already seated at the circular, glass table. Fiona had borrowed the PJs from some kept in the dresser in Naomi's room, and the dressing gown was one of Margaret's.

'Morning!' they said in unison.

'How are you feeling?' asked James.

'Pretty good thanks. All things considered. I can't believe I slept the entire night.'

'I think we all did,' said James, with a knowing smile. 'Don't forget we're meeting the breakdown people this morning. They said they'd call when they're about fifteen minutes away, and that it would be around ten a.m., didn't they?'

'Yes,' said Naomi, pulling out a chair and sitting beside Fiona.

James had called them last night, but as the cover was in her name and registered to her flat in London, they had insisted on speaking with her.

She had also phoned her bank to tell them about her debit card, her credit card company to advise them of the loss of that card, and, having realised that the keys to her flat were also in her handbag, she had called her flatmates to tell them they might need to be on their guard. Or possibly, change the locks.

Not that she thought a mugger who used a bicycle would be likely to travel all the way to London to burgle the flat. And the mugger would have to find her address first anyway. Although she couldn't remember if she had anything in her handbag with her address on. But she was probably being over cautious. And none of them would be living in that flat for very much longer.

Which was something else Naomi needed to discuss with her family.

Now was as good a time as any to tell them she was redundant, and needed to move out of the flat and, if possible, come home until she found another job and another flat.

She waited until they had all consumed a full English breakfast and were munching on toast with marmalade until she broke the news.

'I've got something I need to tell you all. And a huge favour I need to ask. I know you'll say I should've mentioned this sooner, but I didn't want to tell you over the phone – or before the celebratory dinner party, and I wanted to tell you when we were all together.'

'What is it, darling?' Margaret's furrowed brow showed she was anxious and she was no doubt imagining all sorts of dreadful scenarios. 'You know you can tell us anything.'

'I know. And it's nothing that can't be fixed. I hope.'

She told them about her redundancy and why it had come about, due to the building being sold and the café owners having decided to move to Portugal. She had quickly added that they had offered her a job there but that she had naturally refused. She told them of her redundancy pay, which was more than Benedita and John were legally required to give her, and added that yesterday morning had been her last day of work. She was now free to spend each day looking for a new job.

'I have been looking since they told me at the start of the year, but I haven't found anything even remotely suitable yet.'

'You'll find something soon, darling,' said James, reassuringly.

'But if you don't,' said Margaret, squeezing Naomi's hand, 'you might consider moving back here for a while. You know we'd love to have you home.'

'I'm so glad you said that Mum, because that's the favour I needed to ask. May I come home until I find another job? And also a new place to live. You see, the other thing I haven't mentioned is that the landlord has increased our rent starting from the beginning of February to a figure none of us can afford. All three of us are moving out.'

They had all taken the news better than she had expected.

'Of course you can come home,' said Margaret.

'We'll be happy to have you,' said James. 'You can stay for as long as you like.'

'I hope the holdall you brought with you doesn't contain all your worldly goods,' said Fiona.

'Erm. It sort of does. Don't give me that look. The flat was fully furnished. We weren't allowed to hang anything on the walls so I don't have any pictures or anything else like that. And although I loved my job, I didn't earn a fortune so I don't have lots of clothes, or shoes, or jewellery, or stuff. Unlike you. And I've still got some things here, because my bedroom in London was so small and I couldn't fit it all into the flat.'

Now that she had said it, it was rather depressing. She was thirty-three years old and could put virtually everything she owned into one – albeit large – holdall.

'Is there nothing else you need to go back and get?' Margaret also seemed somewhat surprised that Naomi owned so little.

'Not really. I'm a minimalist. I only own what I actually need. But all my books are still here, and all my things from my childhood, along with some clothes I don't wear often, and extra PJs, luckily for Fi.'

Fiona grinned at her. 'I really like these. Any chance I could have them? After all, you've just said you only own what you need. And who needs ten pairs of PJs?'

Naomi tutted. 'I don't have ten pairs.'

'You do. I counted them when you were in the bath and I asked if I could borrow a pair.'

Naomi laughed. 'Gosh. I had no idea I owned so many. And yes. You can keep those.'

'What about ornaments, and photos, and other personal bits and bobs?' asked

63

Margaret.

'I don't have any ornaments in London, only down here in my bedroom. All my photos are on my laptop, which is in the holdall, along with the rest of my personal belongings.' Naomi shrugged. 'Space was at a premium in our flat. The three of us agreed not to clutter it up.'

'Well I suppose it saves us a journey,' said Margaret. 'And it means you won't have to go back to London until you want to.'

'So you've effectively moved back home from today?' Fiona queried. 'Or yesterday, I suppose. Anyway, this means that I don't have to rearrange the dress fitting for next weekend. We can do it any day, can't we? And the celebration dinner doesn't have to be on a Saturday evening now either.'

'Are you thinking of rearranging that?' Naomi asked. 'The wedding itself is only three weeks away.'

'I know. But Greg's mum says that the wedding is all about me. It's my day. She was the one who wanted this celebratory dinner. She said it's for both of us and for all the family, but it's mainly for Greg.' Fiona giggled and shook her head. 'You know what she's like. I just went along with it. And, crazy or not, she wants to rearrange it. Greg told me last night when he called before I went to sleep. He said she's determined to have it, even if it has to be after the wedding.'

'That's a little odd,' said James.

'What can I say, Dad? The whole family is a little odd.'

'This is the man you're about to marry,' said Naomi.

'I know. Love is crazy, isn't it? I love Greg to bits, but as for his family. Not so much.'

'There are a lot of them,' Naomi said, grinning.

'Don't remind me,' laughed Fiona.

'I expect my name was mud last night, for ruining the entire evening.'

'No it wasn't. To be honest, I'm not sure many people noticed you weren't there at first. And when Greg and I told his parents that Mum, Dad, and I had to go, and explained what had happened to you, as best we could with the small amount of info we had, they were actually very concerned about you. Plus, when I spoke to Greg late last night, as well as telling me about the dinner needing to be rearranged, he told me his family want to send you some flowers and asked whether to send them here or to your flat in London. Good thing I said here, isn't it?'

'Wow. They want to send me flowers? Why?'

'Because they see you as part of their family now.'

'Oh joy. Sorry. That was sarcastic. They're lovely people, I know.'

Fiona pulled a face and nodded.

Naomi couldn't quite believe it. Thanks to the mugging and her handbag being stolen, not to mention her car breaking down, Greg and his family had seen her as an innocent victim. No one blamed her for ruining the evening and the dinner that had been so difficult to arrange in the first place.

She felt a little guilty, even though what had happened to her wasn't her fault.

A few hours later, she felt very emotional, when Greg arrived at the cottage to join them for Sunday lunch, and his car was filled to bursting with gifts for her from various members of his family.

There were several bouquets of beautiful flowers, enough boxes of chocolates to last her and her family for a couple of months, and a plethora of bath products to allow them all to take luxuriously relaxing baths for many nights to come. Each gift came with a card wishing her well, and several telling her that if she needed anything at all, she only had to ask.

She was actually moved to tears by their kindness and generosity. It was the second time she had cried today.

The first time was that morning, when her dad had driven her back to her car to meet with the breakdown repair person – who had been a woman – and who had told her that there was nothing she could do to fix the car and that it would need to be towed to a garage in Folkestone.

'I'll be honest,' she had said. 'It's not looking good, and it's going to be expensive. You need a new radiator, for a start, but there are also a few other problems that I can see will need fixing. The whole lot will probably cost far more to repair than the car is worth.'

Naomi had no real affection for the vehicle. A car was just a car. But the thought of not having one when she had owned a car of some sort since she had passed her driving test on her eighteenth birthday and her parents had bought her a second hand Mini, was upsetting. She had fought back her tears as best she could but a few had trickled down her cheeks and she had swiftly wiped them away.

'We'll see what the mechanic says,' James soothed. 'If it has to go for scrap, you can use ours while you're here. And I'm sure your mum and I can help you out financially so that you can get a replacement. Perhaps one a bit younger than this so it might not breakdown so often ... or be so easy to gain access to.'

Naomi smiled. 'Thanks, Dad. But I can't ask you to do that.'

'Then it's just as well I offered, isn't it? Don't be silly sweetheart. You need a car so that, once you do get another job and a flat back in London, you can still pop home and see us whenever you want without needing to rely on public transport.'

'It would be nice to have a slightly more reliable car. Or any car. And I would pay you and Mum back just as soon as I could.'

'Then it's settled. We'll have a look at some this week.'

'I'll get this off to the garage then,' said the breakdown repair woman.

'Could you take it to Boland's, please?' said James. 'The owner is a friend, so I know he'll do right by us.'

'Yep. I can do that. Boland's is one of the places we take a lot of vehicles for repair or scrap. Is there anything in the vehicle you want to take with you?'

'No thanks,' said Naomi. 'We got it all last night.'

She watched as the car was towed away and as she got into her dad's car an odd feeling swept over her. It felt like a door was closing on a part of her life.

She hoped a new one would open up soon.

And that there wouldn't be a gaping big hole on the other side for her to fall into.

Five

The sunshine disappeared not long after lunch, as did Fiona and Greg. Well, they did not disappear exactly; they merely decided it was time they returned to their flat in Folkestone. They both had work the next day and lots of things to do beforehand.

'I'll call you tomorrow,' Fiona said, hugging Naomi tightly. 'I'll rearrange the dress fitting for one day this week. I can leave work early and we can go for a drink and a pizza or something afterwards. Or whatever else you fancy. My treat. You're invited too, Mum. Sadly, Dad, you're not. This is a girl-thing.'

'Excellent news,' said James. 'I can curl up in front of the TV with a beer and a take-away and watch the footie without your mother giving her usual running commentary.' He laughed and winked at his wife.

'I can join you if you like,' ventured Greg.

'Oh. Erm. Yes.' James shot a look at Margaret and then at Fiona, both of whom grinned at him. Naomi gave a little cough and fought back a laugh. He pushed his shoulders back and straightened his torso as if preparing for battle. 'Yes, Greg. Why not? It's about time you and I got to know one another better. After all, you are going to be my son-in-law in two weeks.'

'And I can't wait,' said Greg, with an eager expression on his face, like an enthusiastic puppy.

'Nor can we,' said James, sounding a little less enthusiastic, at least to Naomi's ears.

Her parents both liked Greg, but they often said how different he was from Fiona. She was ambitious and career-driven and had worked her way up the career ladder, adding to her already generous salary along the way and achieving her goal as the youngest head of HR in the history of the company. She worked long hours and often had to deal with disputes between the staff, and even between the staff and the company. She handled sensitive matters, and occasionally had to terminate people's employment. Her job was full-on and highly pressurised.

Greg's ambition was to continue to drive the trains he had loved since he was a kid.

And to get the pay rise he and the fellow members of his union were currently striking for. The union, ASLEF along with the other main union in the transport industry, RMT were seeking better pay and conditions for their members. The train companies maintained that the ways of working needed to change, and the dispute had been ongoing for nineteen months with no end in sight.

Strikers didn't get paid on strike days, but as Fiona earnt almost twice as much as Greg, they weren't suffering any financial hardship, unlike some.

While Fiona's parents supported Greg's endeavours and his love of his job, they did wonder whether he might one day resent the fact that his wife's salary would always exceed his by a substantial amount.

They also wondered what would happen if – or more likely when – Fiona decided she wanted to give up her career and stay at home to bring up the kids they knew she wanted. It would mean a very different lifestyle from the one to which she and Greg were now accustomed.

But on the few occasions Margaret and James, and also Naomi, had broached the subject, after Fiona had announced her engagement, Fiona had dismissed their concerns.

'We'll be fine,' she had said. 'I'm saving

like no one's business so we'll have a nice little nest egg. Plus I can probably work from home a few days a week. Or work part-time. It's not a big deal.'

'It might be a bigger deal than you think,' Margaret had pointed out. 'Marriages crumble over much less than this.'

Fiona had been furious. 'Are you saying you don't think I should marry Greg?'

'No,' said James. 'We're saying you are different people with different ideas of the sort of life you want. Greg loves trains and as long as he can do what he does, he'll be happy, even if it means you must continue living in your flat. You want a house with a garden. Will you be able to afford that when you're living on just Greg's salary?'

'And you want nice cars and clothes and holidays,' Margaret added. 'Will you still be happy if you can't afford those things? Just make sure you're going into this with your eyes wide open, that's all we're saying.'

James had nodded. 'You've only been dating for a year and now you're engaged. Why the rush?'

'Because I love him. And he wants me to be his wife. Which is what I want too. What I don't want is to ever have this conversation or any similar conversations again. I hope that's clear.'

So nothing more was said about it, but it

didn't stop Margaret and James, and even Naomi from wondering. And the closer it got to the wedding, the more the wondering had turned into concern.

Greg was kind and thoughtful and caring and he adored Fiona, that was obvious. He was also extremely handsome, romantic, and sexy. No one could deny him that. If he worked for a bank, or a law firm, or had some other career that meant he might earn a similar salary to Fiona's, would they have the same concerns they had now?

Possibly not.

And yet a bank employee, or a solicitor, or someone with a similar career path might lose their job. They might have faults that Greg did not. They might cheat on Fiona, or hurt her in some other way.

It was not so much a matter of judging Greg on his career choice, as it was a matter of judging Fiona on her choice of life partner. Would Greg make her happy once the glow of what was still a relatively new romance, wore off?

Perhaps they simply did not know Greg as well as Fiona did, and whose fault was that? They needed to spend more time with Greg and really get to know him. That could start with James inviting him round to watch football. Or Naomi taking time to chat with him now that she was in Betancourt Bay for more than just a few days at a time.

'Great,' said Naomi as Fiona got into her car and Greg got into his. 'Let me know the time of the fitting and the day and I'll be there. And I promise you I won't be late.'

Even Greg laughed at that.

'He's a lovely young man,' said James as he, Margaret and Naomi waved them off. 'Yet I can't help but still have some concerns.'

'At least she has someone who adores her,' said Naomi, the green-eyed monster suddenly and unexpectedly rearing its head. 'Oh bloody hell. I don't know where that came from. I must be tired. Would you mind if I took a nap?'

'You don't have to ask,' said Margaret, putting her arm around her daughter as they hurried back inside. 'This is your home too, darling. Do whatever you like.'

Despite having slept all night, Naomi was tired. Perhaps it was the after effects of the shock, not just from yesterday and being mugged, but also from being made redundant, and from having to leave her home of the last few years, and all in such a short space of time.

Yawning as she climbed the stairs, and fighting now to keep her eyes open, she slid beneath her duvet, fully dressed. Perhaps the two glasses of red wine she had consumed with her lunch had made her extra sleepy but the moment her head touched the pillow she could feel herself drifting off to sleep.

Until a thought struck her.

Greg may not earn anything near the amount that Fiona did, but he did have a job ... and a flat ... and a partner. Which was a great deal more than Naomi had.

Were her parents secretly worried about her?

Should they be?

Should she be worried?

She was older than Fiona and yet Fiona was the one who had her life together.

It was time Naomi made some plans.

Time she took control of her future.

Time she fought for what she wanted.

If only she knew what that was.

And if only she knew where to start.

Once again, an image of the handsome stranger she had met in Betancourt Bay Café popped into her head.

But although she would dearly love to see the gorgeous man again, if only to thank him for his help, it wasn't just the memory of his smile and the sparkle in his incredible eyes that set her heart racing, and made her own eyes shoot open as she sat bolt upright on her bed.

It was the image of Betancourt Bay Café.

Six

No longer tired, and feeling invigorated by her thoughts, Naomi took her laptop from her bedside table and began scrolling through images of all the cafés she could find in and around the county of Kent and a little farther afield.

The only money she had was her redundancy pay, and although that wasn't much, if she could find a job fairly fast, she could put that money into a savings account.

Her parents would help in any way they could, so, if this was really possible, she could ask them to lend her the money they were going to give her anyway for a replacement car. She wouldn't need a car if she could pull this off.

But could she actually do it?

And more importantly, would she get the opportunity?

Questions and ideas whirled around in her mind like a cake mix batter. Would this rise and make her proud? Or would it fall flat and make more of a mess than she was in right now?

She could ask the universe for help.

But the last time she had done that, it had sent her a mugger.

She wasn't about to make the same mistake twice.

'Are you awake, darling?' Her mum's voice penetrated her thoughts.

'Yes. Do you need me?'

'Only if you'd like something for tea.'

'For tea?' Naomi glanced at her watch. How could it be six p.m. already? 'I'll be right down.'

She wasn't hungry, but she could murder a cup of tea. Plus, her parents would have gone out earlier for their afternoon walk. They may have met someone who might have an update.

She closed her laptop and slid it under her arm before hurrying downstairs to the kitchen.

'Did you have a good nap?' James asked, sitting in the same seat he had occupied at breakfast.

Lunch was eaten in the dining room, but breakfast, tea and supper were always eaten in the kitchen. Unless the Harts were entertaining guests, in which case every meal was eaten in the dining room.

'I found I couldn't drift off. I did some reading instead. Have you been out for a walk?'

Naomi sat on the chair Fiona had occupied that morning, and even such a small thing as sitting on a different chair, made her smile. New and exciting adventures beckoned, and in order to do something new, she had to do something different.

'We have. It's going to be another cold night, I think, but not as windy as last night.'

'Did you speak to anyone from the village?'

James gave her a curious look as Margaret placed a large cup of tea in front of him, and one in front of Naomi.

'No. Why? There's a strange look on your face, sweetheart. Anything you want to share?'

Naomi smiled. 'No. Not yet. Just a few things whirling around in my mind.' She lifted the cup to her lips but let it hover there, holding it with both hands. 'So no news about what's happened with Doris and Derek?'

Margaret shook her head. 'No. But we did stroll up to the café and there's now a sign on the glass door saying, "Closed until further notice due to unforeseen circumstances." I don't know if that means they've been arrested, they've decided they can no longer work together, or they're selling the business, as you said Derek threatened.'

'Or perhaps they're trying to sort things out,' suggested James, reaching for a chocolate éclair from the plate of various cakes and pastries in the centre of the glass table. 'Those two have been throwing unpleasant remarks at one another for years.'

'They were throwing more than unpleasant remarks yesterday, Dad.'

'That's true. It was about time that man stood up for himself.' He bit into the éclair and cream oozed from each side. 'This is delicious.'

Naomi nodded and reached for one herself. Fortunately there were three éclairs on the plate, so that meant one for each of them.

'It's weird how two people who clearly make one another miserable, can stay together for so long and then suddenly one little thing happens and it blows up and all comes crashing down.'

'I wouldn't call you being mugged, and Doris refusing to help, 'one little thing', darling,' Margaret said, sounding irritated at the thought and squeezing the éclair she took so hard that the cream shot out onto the table.

They all laughed as James stretched forward and wiped it up with his fingers and then licked the cream from them.

'No. Nor would I really. But you know what I mean.'

'I think most of the locals will be hoping the Dunpoles do sell up,' said Margaret. 'It would be lovely to have some pleasant people running that café. Other than the pub, and going into Folkestone, or one another's homes as we all do now, there's nowhere we can meet for a coffee and a chat. It would be good to have the café to pop into.'

Naomi brightened at the thought.

'It is still part of the Betancourt Estate, isn't it? I mean the Betancourts own the freehold, don't they, and the Dunpoles have a long lease? From what Derek said, that doesn't have many years left to run. What do you think the Betancourts will do if the Dunpoles leave? Will a new long lease be granted to someone else? Or perhaps they'll opt for a shorter lease, in case the new people are as awful as the Dunpoles?'

'No idea,' said James. 'Grace might know. Now that she and Griff Betancourt are dating. Now that's something none of us saw coming.' He chuckled between sips of tea.

'And yet,' said Margaret, 'they are clearly so well suited. And head over heels in love.

That's a match made in heaven if ever I saw one. I feel sorry for Russell. But what was he thinking? As if Hope would be likely to date him. He's lovely, but he's not her type at all. Then again, they say we can't choose who we fall in love with. Although I chose you, my love.' She blew James a kiss. 'The moment I saw you I knew I was going to be your wife.'

'And I chose you, my angel.' He blew her a kiss right back.

'Oh please,' laughed Naomi. 'Daughter present. Single daughter, I might add.'

'Is Russell your type?' James joked.

'Not really. The handsome stranger in the café was though.'

'Who?' Margaret asked.

'Oops! I hadn't meant to say that out loud. Erm. The man who was in Betancourt Bay Café yesterday when you arrived. The one I told you bought me a hot chocolate and let me use his phone.'

'Oooh,' said Margaret, stringing out the word. 'You liked him, did you? Why didn't you ask him for his name and number then?'

'That's the question I've been asking myself ever since,' Naomi said. 'I'll probably never see him again.'

'You never know,' said James, reaching out for another cake, this time a sugar coated jam doughnut. 'The universe works in mysterious ways.'

'You don't need to tell me that!' Naomi groaned. 'I asked it to send me someone after my car broke down yesterday. And what did I get? A mugger.'

'Oh goodness me.' James shook his head. 'Perhaps you need to be careful what you wish for. Or possibly, just be more specific.'

'I agree,' said Margaret. 'So if you want to see the handsome stranger again, you must ask specifically for the man who bought you the hot chocolate in Betancourt Bay Café, and let you use his phone. If you only ask to see the handsome stranger again, the mugger might return. And we wouldn't want that. Muggers may be horribly unpleasant people, but they can be handsome too, don't you think?'

Naomi snorted out a strangled laugh. 'I don't know, Mum! But if I ever do ask the universe for help again, I'll definitely be exceedingly careful what I wish for.'

Seven

Naomi was nodding off on the sofa when the landline rang around ten, and a few moments later, her mum handed her the phone.

'It's Grace,' Margaret said, smiling. 'I told her you were okay to talk.'

Naomi took the phone, mouthing her thanks to her mum.

'Grace! Hi. I was going to call you myself either this evening, but I nodded off on the sofa. How are you?'

'Hi, Naomi. Me? I'm fine, thanks. Better than fine. But how are you? I'm sorry to bother you so late on a Sunday evening, but Griff and I were away this weekend and we've only just got home and heard about what happened to you.'

'I'm okay, thanks. Just a little shocked and a bit bruised, that's all. Did you go somewhere nice?'

'We went to stay with Griff's friend,

Davina.'

'Wasn't she the one you told me about? The one you thought was his girlfriend?'

'Yes.' Grace laughed. 'You'll have to meet her one day. She's fantastic. But tell me about you. Are you really okay? Is there anything you need? Or anything we can do?'

Naomi sat upright. 'Actually, Grace. There is. I need a chat if possible whenever you have a moment to spare. I know how busy you are with the family business, but if you have time for a coffee or a glass of wine, or even just a walk, one day this week, that would be great.'

'Oh. Yes. Of course,' Grace sounded pleased but surprised. 'You're right. We're constantly busy these days, more so after the massive success of the Mistletoe Dance, but we're not complaining. And I can always make time for a chat with a dear friend. I'll need to quickly check in with Mum and everyone, just to be sure, but whenever suits you is fine with me. Shall I call them and then get back to you? Or if you're free tomorrow morning I can come round and see you about nine-ish. I know I don't have anything in my schedule for then, and I'll be seeing the family at eight, so I can come to you right after that.'

'That would be perfect, Grace. Thank you. Oh, and how is Granny Joy?'

'She's doing well, thanks. The treatment seems to be working although it's early days. Griff arranged for her to see a specialist the Betancourts know, last week, just to get a second opinion, and thankfully he agrees with the prognosis, so fingers crossed.'

'That's good news. So ... have you moved in with Griff, then? You said you'll be seeing the family at eight, and that sounds as if you're not living in The White House now.'

Grace laughed. 'Nothing ever gets past you, does it? Yes and no. I do spend most nights here with Griff, but I still officially live at Mum and Dad's. Between you and me, he has said he would love it if I would move in permanently, especially as he lives here now and rarely spends time at his place in London. He goes up to town for work from time to time but mostly he stays in contact with the office remotely, and via Russell of course. But strictly speaking, Betancourt is still his dad's house even if Griff is the one who now runs it. And Bianca's still here. As much as I love Griff, and as huge as this place is, it's still not big enough for me and Bianca. She does try to be nicer these days, but she is constantly reminding me that I thought I was in love with Russell for most of my life. And although she's no longer drinking, she can be as unpleasant as she always was with anyone who crosses her path. Griff says he has a plan, but he won't tell me what that is, so we'll have to wait and see. Sorry.' She laughed again. 'I was calling to see how you are. Not to drone on about me and my love life.'

'A love life? What's that? Remind me?'

'Still no one making your heart sing?'

'No. Well ... there was one man who made every part of me sing. But it was only for a moment and I don't know who he is, where he lives, or even if he's single. I'll probably never see him again either, so I don't know why I mentioned him. Except, I can't seem to get him out of my head.'

'Oooh. That sounds interesting. But how come you don't know his name? Or anything about him?'

'Don't laugh. It's because he was in Betancourt Bay Café yesterday and he bought me a hot chocolate, and let me use his phone. Oh, and he saved me from crashing to the floor when I sort of fainted.'

'Fainted?'

'Yes. But it was because I'd walked in the freezing cold from where my car broke down, across the fields to the café, and all with a broken heel, and getting mugged along the way.'

'Wait ... let me get this straight. You're saying this man was in the café and he came to your aid, like a knight in shining armour?'

'In jeans, a polo shirt and a jumper, to be precise, but yes. And he was to die for, Grace. I mean, unbelievably hot. His eyes were the most stunning eyes I've ever seen and his voice! Phwoar is all I can say.'

'Wow. Doesn't anyone else know who he is?'

'Derek, Doris, the handsome stranger and I were the only ones in the café. Until my family arrived, followed shortly after by the police. They know who he is but they're not telling. The police that is, not my family. I haven't spoken to anyone in the village so I suppose someone here might know him. I do intend to ask around, because I'd really like to thank him, apart from anything else. But what do I say? Do you know a handsome man who was in Betancourt Bay Café on Saturday evening, and if so, who he is, and how can I get in touch with him?'

'That sounds as good a place as any to start. I'll tell Hope and the rest of my family to ask around. And Griff might know someone who can find out things.'

'Like a private investigator, you mean? Thanks but I can't afford that, Grace. I've just been made redundant. And I'm moving home because I can no longer afford the rent on the flat in London, so a P.I. is way out of my price range.'

'Oh my God, Naomi! You've really been

going through it haven't you? And then for the car to break down and you to get mugged. That's a lot of bad luck. Hopefully you'll only have good luck from now on. As for the P.I. thing, I wasn't suggesting you employ one. Griff has friends in all sorts of places doing all sorts of jobs. If he doesn't know a P.I. himself then he'll know someone who does. And he'll pay. I know him well enough to know that. But it's late, so I'll let you get to bed. I just wanted to call to check you're okay.'

'I ... I don't know what to say.'

'Say, good night, Grace, and I'll see you tomorrow,' Grace said, with laughter in her voice.

'Good night, Grace, and I'll see you tomorrow.'

'Good night, Naomi,' said Grace. 'And pleasant dreams.'

Eight

Grace arrived at Sunnycliff Cottage at nine on the dot on Monday morning, bringing cakes and croissants, and a huge bouquet of flowers.

'Thank you so much for these,' Naomi said when Margaret showed Grace into the sitting room, after taking her coat and hanging it in the hall.

'You're most welcome,' said Grace giving Naomi a gentle hug, clearly not wanting to hurt her in case she was still bruised after the mugging.

'I'll put the flowers in a vase,' said Margaret, 'and bring in some plates. I was going to make you both a pot of coffee. Unless you'd prefer tea, Grace?'

'Coffee is perfect, thanks,' Grace said, putting the box of cakes and bag of croissants on the coffee table. 'I've brought enough for everyone, so please help yourself.'

'Thank you, Grace.' Margaret smiled.

'Sit wherever you like,' said Naomi who was on the sofa, surrounded by sheets of paper, and her laptop. 'It's lovely to see you again.'

'And you.' Grace made a beeline for the chair beside the wood burner. 'It's freezing out there again this morning. I wouldn't be at all surprised if we get more snow. But I have news. Don't get too excited, but Griff does know a man who knows a man who might be able to help. Of course we don't have much to go on, so if you can describe your handsome stranger, and any distinguishing features you can recall about him, other than him being hot,' Grace laughed. 'That would be great.'

'I'll do my best. And thank you. Please thank Griff too.'

'He wanted to come with me but I told him we needed some girl-time. So, is there something in particular you want to talk about? Or was it just a general chat you wanted?'

Naomi leant forward. 'This is a bit awkward, and I don't want you to feel in any way that you have to go along with this, or tell me anything, just because we're friends, but am I right in thinking the Betancourts still own the freehold of Betancourt Bay Café?'

Grace was clearly taken aback. 'Oh. Erm. Yes. As far as I know. At least they did. I can ask Griff if they still do. Why do you want to know about that?'

'Did you hear about the row the Dunpoles had?'

Grace nodded. 'Yes. Tabby told Griff and me about it last night, after she told us about what happened to you. I suspect the entire village is talking about it.'

'Well, during that row, Derek said that the long lease they have on the café didn't have many years left to run. He also said he was thinking of selling up. I ... I'd like to know if that's true. And whether or not he was serious about selling. It might have just been something he said in the heat of the moment, but I'm assuming, if the Betancourts own the freehold, he'll have to tell Griff if that's his plan.'

'Erm. Yes. I suppose he would. I'll have to ask Griff. But ... why the sudden interest in the café?'

Naomi hesitated for a moment when there was a knock on the sitting room door.

'It's only me,' trilled Margaret who came in with a tray on which there was a large pot of coffee, milk and sugar, two plates, and two of the best mugs. She placed it on the coffee table.

'Thanks, Mum.'

'You're welcome. Call if you need anything else.'

'Thank you, Mrs Hart,' said Grace.

'Please, Grace. I'm always telling you to call me Margaret.'

Grace laughed. 'I know. Mum is always telling Naomi to call her Pat, and yet neither of us feel we're grown up enough to call you and Mum by your Christian names. It's weird, isn't it?'

Margaret grinned. 'No. We all do it. I still struggle to call some of the older villagers by their Christian names. Right. I'll leave you to do the honours, darling.' She nodded towards the coffee pot, smiled at Naomi and then Grace, and left them to it.

Naomi sat further forward on the sofa, poured the coffee and handed a mug to Grace.

'Help yourself to milk and sugar.'

'Thanks. And you help yourself to those.' Grace nodded at the pastries.

Naomi put a Belgian bun on a plate, sat back a little and took a bite.

'Belgian buns are one of my favourites,' she said, swallowing the first mouthful.

'Mine too. I love anything with icing. And the more icing the better.'

'Same here.' Naomi took another bite, and washed it down with a swig of coffee. 'Okay. You asked why I'm interested in the café. Here's the thing. I told you last night that I've just been made redundant because the café I managed was closing. The owners offered me a job at their new place, but it's in Portugal.'

'Blimey. That would be a long commute,' Grace joked. 'I take it you're not moving to Portugal?'

'No. But I have moved back here because the rent on the flat in London has been increased and none of us can afford it, especially as I'm not working. It was only going to be temporary while I looked for a new job, and then I'd find another flat in London and move back. That was the plan. Now I'm not so sure. The thing is ... I've always wanted to have my own café one day, but I never dreamt it would really be possible. And perhaps it still isn't. But, the handsome stranger isn't the only thing I can't get out of my head. I'm now wondering if there is even the slightest possibility that Betancourt Bay Café may soon become available. And if it does, whether there is any way that I could afford to buy what is left of the lease. Or enter into a new arrangement with the owners. This is strictly business, Grace, and if Griff isn't interested, or doesn't think it'll work. Or has other plans, that's fine. Obviously. But I had to ask or I'd never forgive myself.'

'Oh I see. Erm. This is a bit of a surprise. I do know that the Dunpoles haven't told Griff anything as yet, because if they had, I'm sure Griff would've mentioned it, especially when Tabby told us about the row and everything. But they may contact him today.' Grace studied Naomi's face for a second. 'You're serious about this, aren't you?'

Naomi nodded. 'Yes. I know it's a long shot, and I'll completely understand if Griff says no right away, but there's no harm in asking, right?'

'Hmm. I should've let Griff come with me after all.' Grace lifted her mug to her lips, and drank.

'You're not cross, are you? I haven't overstepped our friendship, have I?'

Grace almost choked, and she quickly put her mug on the coffee table and cleared her throat.

'Don't be silly! Of course not. I was just thinking, that's all.' Grace smiled reassuringly at Naomi. 'Now. What we need to know first is if the Betancourts still own the café. That's easily solved. I'll call Griff and ask.' She took her phone from her handbag and pressed the screen.

'Wait! You haven't heard the rest of it. The only money I have is my redundancy and that's not much.'

Grace held her forefinger in the air. 'Hi gorgeous. Do you have a second? I need to ask you something. Does your family still own the freehold of Betancourt Bay Café?'

Grace smiled down the phone but Naomi could not hear what Griff was saying. 'Yes I know it seems like a strange question, but bear with me. Yes or no? Or would you rather not discuss your family's business affairs with me? I understand if you'd rather not.' She met Naomi's anxious look with another smile and after a second, nodded her head and held her thumb up. 'Aww. And I love you too. That's great news. Thanks. I'll explain when I see you. Oh wait! Have the Dunpoles contacted you about selling up?' Now Grace laughed. 'I've always been weird. But yes, I know it's another odd question. They haven't? Damn! Oh well. Will you let me know if they do?' She shot a look at Naomi. 'Yes. I'm with Naomi. And yes. This does have something to do with her. I'll tell you when I see you. Love you more than I ever thought possible. Bye-ee!' She blew three kisses into the phone and ended the call.

'He wasn't cross was he?'

'Cross? No. Not at all. He was laughing. But he does think I'm behaving weirdly. Anyway. Yes. The Betancourts still own the freehold. But no. He hasn't heard from the Dunpoles. He will let me know if he does though. What were you saying about money?'

Naomi let out a sigh. 'I don't have any. Apart from a few thousand pounds of redundancy money. Dad said he and Mum will buy me another car, so I can ask them to lend me that cash to go towards the café lease instead. But it won't be much. Oh. And I'll get my share of the deposit money on the flat, returned. So there's that. It really depends on how many years are left on the lease and how much it might go for. Assuming Derek was serious, that is. And we don't know that as yet.'

'Griff will know the remaining term. And he'll probably have a pretty good idea of the market value. But you're right. The person we really need to speak to is Derek Dunpole. Or his lovely wife.' Grace's voice dripped sarcasm as she grinned at Naomi.

Naomi grinned back. 'Those two are enough to put anyone off marriage. Mum said there's a sign on the café door saying that it's closed until further notice. I know they live in Folkestone but I have no idea where. I'm not sure anyone in the village will know because the Dunpoles weren't exactly liked, were they? Although Barbra Brimble was very friendly with Doris, so Mum says. Barbra may know how to contact them. But I can't really ask her to let me have their address so that I can find out if the Dunpoles do intend to sell up, can I? She and the Dunpoles will probably just tell me to mind my own business. And who would blame them?'

'Griff will know where they live. It'll be on the lease. And he can contact them and say he's heard they may want to sell. As the freeholder, he, or whoever does that stuff for the family, will have to give consent for any sale or transfer of the lease, so that's a perfectly valid question, coming from him.'

'Wow. Would he do that?'

Grace shrugged. 'I can ask him. I don't see why he wouldn't. Although ... he might say it was an invasion of privacy, I suppose, and he'd prefer not to. I can work on him.' She grinned broadly. 'And I'd certainly enjoy trying to persuade him.' The grin slowly slid from her lips. 'There's only one problem. What if the Dunpoles don't intend to sell? What if they make up and decide to continue as they were? The remaining term of the lease could be anything from a year to several years.'

'Oh. Oddly enough I hadn't really thought of that.' Naomi let out another sigh. 'I'd need to find a job and a place to live, and just bide my time, I suppose. I mean, they'll have to retire eventually. I'll need to make sure I'm there when they do.'

'So you're really serious about this café then? No matter what?'

Naomi nodded. 'Yes. I am. It's the perfect place for me. I'll admit it only occurred to me yesterday, but I've always thought it would be great to have that café. It just never entered my head that it might be available one day. It's time I followed my dreams, and having made the decision that the café is what I want, all I've thought about since, is how I might be able to make that happen. I know this might sound crazy but somehow it just feels right.'

'That doesn't sound crazy at all. I believed for years that I was in love with Russell. When I realised it was Griff I was really in love with it, I thought I was going crazy. And yet it felt so right. He feels so right. We feel so right together. Sometimes it takes a while. Maybe even years. But when you know, you just know.'

'Yes! That's it. The moment I realised that Betancourt Bay Café was what I wanted, it felt so right. As if it's been sitting there just waiting for me to realise. Of course the reality of me actually getting it might prove more difficult than I hope, but if it's really meant to be then it will be. Won't it?'

'Yes. But if it doesn't happen right away … I mean if it turns out that it might take a while for that to happen, what then? You'd definitely like to stay in Betancourt Bay?'

'Yes. If that's possible. I'll miss London and my friends, of course, but not as much as I always missed Betancourt Bay and my family when I was living in London. And my friends can visit if I'm here.'

Grace's brows furrowed. 'You want a job?'

'I know. But I can still dream about owning Betancourt Bay Café one day.'

'No. That was a question, not a statement. Although it could be both. I'll have to check with the others but I know they'll agree. We are so busy now and we've been talking about employing more people to help. Why don't you come and work for us? The hours can be flexible if you still want to find work in a café as well. But the pay will be competitive, and I think we're pretty nice people to work for.'

'Are you ... are you offering me a job with Eversley Events? Seriously?'

'Yes. It's not what you're used to, I know, but you'll soon learn the ropes. And organising an event is a bit like running a café. With a few extras. Or, if you'd rather, you can do some baking for us. We have suppliers and caterers we trust, but we always need more. Have a think about it and let me know.'

'I ... I don't need to think about it, Grace! Yes. Yes please. I'd love to work for you and your family. Oh. Assuming they agree. And if they don't, that's fine. I understand.'

Grace burst out laughing. 'Will you stop

doing that? Will you stop thinking that there's a definite chance people won't want you. I'll call them now and you'll see.'

'I can't help it,' said Naomi. 'I'm not exactly the sort of person people are dying to employ. Or to date. Or anything.'

Grace tutted, picked up her phone, pressed the screen, and a second or two later, had an answer for Naomi.

'Well that's where you're wrong. Because you are the sort of person we are dying to employ. Mum just said so. Welcome to Eversley Events. When would you like to start?'

Nine

'It's me,' said Fiona, when Naomi answered the landline, still buzzing from the news she'd received that morning. 'How's your day been so far?'

'It's been brilliant. I've called and left you a couple of messages.'

'I know. Which is why I'm calling you now. I've been stuck in meetings all morning and I've only just got them. I was worried something awful had happened when I saw you'd called and just said, "ring me as soon as you can" – twice. But clearly something good has happened, so that's a relief. Tell me your news.'

'I've got a new job.'

'What? That was quick. Well done. Erm. In London?'

'No. Here. In Betancourt Bay. I'm working for Eversley Events.'

'Eversley...? Are you serious? Wow. Congratulations. When do you start?'

'Thank you. I'm helping at events from next Monday but I'm actually starting work tomorrow. I'm going to be baking for them this week and learning what's involved with event planning. Under the terms of their insurance, because I've been involved in 'an incident' after which I sort of fainted, I need to see a doctor to get a clean bill of health. Luckily, Grace has pulled some strings and got me an appointment for Thursday with a GP in a private practice. I think Griff may have helped but she didn't say. Anyway, it's not going to cost me anything, thank goodness. And before you worry about rearranging the bridesmaid dress fitting, my hours are flexible, so just tell me when.'

'Phew. Because I've also had a message confirming that it's rescheduled for this Wednesday at four-thirty. I know I don't have to say, please don't be late. But I'll say it anyway. Please don't be late.' Fiona laughed.

'I won't. I'll make a note of it right now. I'm writing it on the pad beside the phone, as we speak. You did say five, didn't you?' Naomi teased.

'No! I said ... oh you're hilarious. I'd better go because it's manic here today. I'll speak to you later and I'll see you on Wednesday, if not before. Congratulations again and good luck for tomorrow. Not that you'll need it. Your baking is superb.'

'Wow. Thank you. See you on Wednesday. I'll be there on the dot of five.'

'Stop it. Or you'll convince yourself it is five, and you will be late. Goodbye.'

Fiona was probably right. Naomi wrote another note only this time she wrote a huge number four and drew arrows all around it.

She also wrote a note for the kitchen and she was sticking it on the fridge with a dolphin shaped magnet when her parents came home. They had popped out to the shops an hour before, saying they needed a few bits and bobs.

'We're home, darling!' her mum called from the hall. 'Oh. I see Fiona's rearranged the dress fitting.'

'Yep. I'm in the kitchen sticking a note on the fridge. Shall I put the kettle on?'

'Will it fit you?' her dad called out.

'Funny. The old ones are always the best. And so are the old jokes. Would you like me to make you a hot beverage?'

James popped his head around the door and grinned from ear to ear.

'Yes please, sweetheart. And would you like to see the little gift your mum and I have just bought you?'

Naomi nearly dropped the kettle.

Please don't let them have bought me a car, she silently begged the universe.

She took a deep breath and forced a

smile.

'A gift? For me? Oh yes please. But you shouldn't have.'

It would have to be a very tiny car. The bag James was waving in the air in the kitchen doorway was about the size of an average paperback book.

Had they bought her a book?

'We hope you like it.' Margaret looked more excited than Naomi felt. 'You'll need it for your new job.'

A cook book? Had they bought her a small cook book? Or a dairy? Or an events planner?

There was only one way to find out.

She walked towards the door and they met her halfway. James was grinning like a Cheshire Cat as he handed her the bag. She tried to look as pleased as she took a peek inside.

Her head shot up and she stared at her parents in disbelief. She had instantly recognised the rectangular black box inside the bag because she'd seen it enough times in the TV adverts.

'Oh my God! Thank you, so, so much.'

Now she quickly removed the box and, setting it gently on the kitchen table, she opened the lid as if it contained something precious. Which it did. It contained a brand new mobile phone.

'I don't know why we didn't buy you one for Christmas,' said Margaret. 'Your phone was so old. But you always said it was fine.'

'Just as well we didn't,' James said. 'If we had, a certain mugger would be very happy right now.'

'Good point,' said Margaret. 'Do you like it, darling? Is it the right one? The man in the store said we could change it if we took it back today. We bought it outright so there's no contract. We've bought a new sim card and you need to sort out an airtime plan and get your number transferred. We'll pay for that but we wanted you to decide what you want.'

'I absolutely love it! I don't know what to say.' Naomi threw her arms around each of her parents and kissed them both on their cheeks. 'You are the best parents ever. But a cheaper phone would've been just as good. You didn't need to go to this expense.'

'You're worth every penny, sweetheart,' James said. 'And we'll still buy you that car, so don't you worry about that. We're paying for most of Fiona's wedding, so it's only right you have some money spent on you. We've been saving for years for anything you two girls might need.'

'Oh, Dad. You don't know what this means to me. Thank you from the bottom of my heart. But about that car. Erm. I'd rather not rush into anything, if that's okay with you.'

James looked confused, but he nodded. 'Of course. Whatever you want is fine with us. We can talk about that another time. Let's get this phone and the airtime plan set up and then you can start letting people know you've got a mobile phone again.'

'That would be great. But ... what you said about Fiona's wedding just now. Does that mean you think I won't be getting married?'

'What?' James laughed out loud. 'No. We've got money for your wedding too. And when that day comes – and it will – we'll buy Fiona something nice, just as we're doing for you now.'

Naomi let out a dramatic sigh of relief and laughed. 'For a moment there, I thought you might be trying to tell me something.'

The thought that she might not fall in love and marry had crossed her mind several times, especially when Fiona announced her engagement. So she was pleased her parents still believed there was hope for her in the romance department.

And she had no idea why, but since she'd seen that handsome stranger in Betancourt Bay Café, she had begun to believe it herself. There was something in his eyes when he had looked at her. And something in that gorgeous smile.

Now all she had to do was find him, and see where things went from there.

Ten

After spending the whole of Tuesday, and most of Wednesday baking, with assistance from her mum, Naomi was happier than she had been for a long time.

She had a new job, a new phone, a comfortable home, albeit her parents' house, and a good friend less than two minutes' walk away.

She had been able to video call her friends in London – something she could never do with her old phone, and they had been thrilled for her when she had told them her news. Along with her decision to remain in Betancourt Bay.

'You're welcome to come and visit any time you want,' she told them. 'Mum and Dad have told me they don't mind at all. And I'd love you to see the café I've got my sights set on. Whether I get it or not depends on many factors but at least now I have a plan for my future.'

They had asked her to send them photos of the café and had promised to pay her a visit as soon as they could.

She had also now told her parents and Fiona of her dream to own Betancourt Bay Café, when Fiona had popped round on Tuesday evening and the time had just felt right.

'There's something I want to tell you all,' she had said as they sat around the circular, kitchen table. 'I've been speaking to Grace about Betancourt Bay Café and it seems the Betancourts still own the freehold. The Dunpoles haven't been in contact with Griff about selling or transferring the lease yet, so I don't know what their plans are, but I do know that whatever happens, I'd like to try to take over the lease from them if they do sell. Or purchase a new lease from the Betancourts when the Dunpole's lease expires, assuming Derek and Doris decide to retire. I'll have to wait and see what happens but I wanted you all to know that I'm making plans. I've always wanted to have my own café, and having one in Betancourt Bay would be a dream come true.'

All three of them were surprised but elated.

Margaret beamed at her. 'Oh darling! That is wonderful news. You know your dad and I will help you in any way we can. Wait.

Is this why you wanted to hold off on the car? Are you hoping to use that money towards the lease of the café instead? Because if you are that's fine by us. Although, depending on how much it is, we might be able to sort something out. We'd love to have you home again permanently. And for you to have your own business here would be fantastic.'

'Actually, Mum, yes it was. I was going to ask you and Dad but I was hoping to hear something about the Dunpoles first. I've got my redundancy money, and I'll have the money from my returned deposit on the flat, once that comes through. Plus now I'm working, I can save some money from my pay. Although I would like to contribute something towards the bills for this cottage as I'm living here right now.'

'Don't give that another thought,' said James. 'We don't need money towards the bills and we'd far rather you add that to your savings to set yourself up for the future. And we'll let you have as much as possible. Once you know what is happening, and we have some idea of the sums involved, we can discuss it in more detail.'

'You and Mum are the best. I love you both so much.'

'And we love you, darling.'

'What about me?' asked Fiona.

'Sorry sweetheart? What do you mean?

Are you asking if we love you too? Surely you know we do?'

Fiona gave a snort of laughter. 'No! Of course I know you love me. And I wasn't talking to you or Mum. I was asking Naomi. I've got money I can invest if you'd like a silent partner. Not a lot, but some. I know there's a risk involved with all new businesses but the café has been there for years and with the right person running it, it could be a little gold mine, I'm sure of that.'

'I agree,' said Naomi. 'And I'll take money from anyone who is willing to give it, so yes. If you're sure. And if it does go wrong, I'll spend the rest of my life repaying every penny. Not that it will go wrong. The only problem is when I can get started.'

'Couldn't someone ask the Dunpoles what they intend to do?' said Fiona.

Naomi nodded. 'Griff is going to get in touch with them and say he's heard a rumour and just wondered if there was anything he could do. That way, if they're hanging on because they're unsure what to do, it might be the spur to motivate them.'

'I'm impressed,' said James. 'It seems you've got it all planned out.'

'Grace has been helping me. I'm not sure Griff would do this if I asked him. He's doing it for her, not me. Although he did tell her that he'd be happy to have a chat with me about the café and the future, so fingers crossed. We're going to wait and see what the Dunpoles say to him, and then we'll have that chat.'

Now Naomi was getting ready to go and meet Fiona at the Bridal shop for the final fitting, and she already had more good news to share concerning Betancourt Bay Café.

'I'll just empty the tumble dryer,' Margaret said, heading towards the kitchen, 'and then we can be on our way.'

'Okay. I'll get my coat on so that I'm ready. I don't want to be late.' Naomi laughed as she walked into the hall and grabbed her coat from the rack.

'Get mine down too, please, darling,' Margaret called out from the kitchen.

'Already have, Mum.'

Naomi shrugged on her coat and slipped her hand into the pocket in search of her gloves, surprised as something cool touched her skin.

A two pound coin?

She stared at it as she held it between her fingers. Where had that...?

Oh. Of course! That night. That awful – and yet equally magical – night last week.

She had not worn this coat since then because she had not been out of the cottage. She was wearing it today because it was freezing out again, and the only other coat she possessed was actually not a coat at all. It was a leather jacket. But today was definitely a winter coat day. Just like the day she had been mugged.

She had tried not to think about the mugging and the fear that had swept over her as the cyclist had barrelled towards her. The police officers who had taken her statement had since been in touch – this very morning in fact – to say their enquiries were ongoing but there was little to no chance of catching the thief who had stolen her handbag. Or of recovering her items. They would lct her know if there were any further developments. She did not expect she would hear from them again.

Since Saturday night, she had tried to remember only the good bits. The fact that it was the night she had met the man of her dreams. Only to lose him ... for the time being.

Now she had found that coin she was asking herself for the umpteenth time, why she hadn't asked the handsome stranger for his name.

She might have forgotten about the two pound coin but she had not forgotten him.

She had dreamt about him each night since, and although it had only been four nights ago, it already felt like it was an eternity since she had seen him. Would she ever see those gorgeous eyes again? Or that wonderful smile? Or hear that deep but oh so sexy voice?

'Look what I've found. Again.' Naomi laughed as she wandered into the kitchen to show the coin to her mum. 'I haven't worn this coat since that night and I completely forgot about this coin in all the drama.'

'You should use it to buy a Lottery ticket,' Margaret said. 'I'm buying one for us today.'

'That's what Doris Dunpole told me to do with it that night.' Naomi looked at the coin and smiled.

Margaret shook her head. 'We don't usually buy them, because the chances of winning are pretty slim, even for the smallest prize, but it's one of those, 'Must be won' draws tonight. The jackpot can only rollover so many times, and then it must be won. And if no one wins the jackpot tonight, then the money rolls down so that each prize is worth more. The chances of winning don't increase, but if you do win something, it'll be more than the usual amount.'

'Perhaps I will buy one then. Although I'm not usually lucky, so perhaps I should just add it to my savings.'

Margaret slid the laundry basket which was full to the brim with fluffy towels, over to one side and chuckled.

'Buy that Lottery ticket, darling. You

never know. Your luck does seem to be changing. Perhaps you found that two pound coin for a reason.'

Naomi considered Margaret's words. Things had certainly improved for her since that night.

Perhaps her mum was right? Perhaps her luck was changing. She had found that two pound coin. And had fallen in love at first sight with a handsome stranger.

Since then she had been given a brand new phone. She had also been given a job. Tonight she was getting a free meal thanks to her sister.

Maybe finding the coin again today was a sign. Perhaps she would win something on the 'Must be won' Lottery tonight?

Would she also be lucky enough to see the handsome stranger again?

Naomi snorted a laugh as she dropped the coin back into her pocket.

Was that a pig flying past the window?

As if her luck would ever change that much.

Eleven

'The traffic's blooming awful,' said the driver of the cab Naomi and Margaret had ordered to take them into Folkestone.

Normally Margaret would have driven but as they were going out for pizza after the dress fitting and would therefore be having a glass or two of wine, they decided to take a cab.

James had offered to take them but Margaret had done quite a lot of online shopping and was expecting several deliveries to arrive today.

'It'll be Sod's Law that they all arrive the moment we leave the house,' she had said.

'But it'll only take a few minutes for me to get there and back,' James had replied.

'Yes. And it only takes a few minutes for a delivery driver to decide no one's home, and then who knows when the parcels will arrive? We'll get a cab.'

'It's a good thing your dad didn't bring

us,' said Margaret now. 'Those few minutes have already been fifteen.'

'Pot holes,' said the driver.

'I beg your pardon?'

'Pot holes,' he repeated. 'That's what's causing these jams. The council puts those stupid cones over them and then some silly sods knock the cones flying and now there's not only a hole in the road to avoid, there's a bloody cone to drive around too.'

'How long do you think we'll be?' Naomi asked, shooting a look at her watch. 'I can't be late. I simply can't.'

He glanced at her via the rear view mirror. 'Can't perform miracles, love. We'll get there when we get there. I'm doing my best, but my name's not Moses. I can't part the traffic and drive through.'

He laughed at his comment but Naomi didn't find it amusing. She must not be late. She had promised.

She glanced around from the back seat trying to decide if they could get to the Bridal shop faster on foot than he could drive there. They couldn't run. She was wearing her recently mending favourite boots and the last time she wore those she broke the heel.

The driver stopped abruptly and honked his horn. 'Bloody cyclists. They shouldn't be allowed on the road.'

'Or the pavement,' Naomi said, without

thinking.

She watched the cyclist weave in and out of the traffic, narrowly missing a pedestrian who had had the audacity to cross the road on an actual pedestrian crossing. Cyclists didn't seem to believe they should stop for those.

And then her heart skipped a beat.

It was him.

'Mum!' she said, reaching out and grabbing Margaret's arm. 'It's him.'

Margaret darted a look in the direction of her daughter's. 'The cyclist? Oh my goodness. The mugger! That's the person who–'

'No! Not the cyclist. The man who just crossed the road. Look. Right there.'

Naomi pointed at the back of a tall, broad shouldered man with short brown hair who was wearing jeans and a black coat and had just stepped onto the pavement.

'Your handsome stranger?' Margaret stared at him in disbelief.

'Stop!' Naomi yelled, as the traffic suddenly eased and the cab quickly moved forward. 'I need to get out here.'

'What?' the driver asked. 'I thought you were in a hurry and couldn't be late.'

Naomi hesitated for just a second. If she got out here and followed the stranger, she would definitely be late for the dress fitting.

But if she didn't get out here, she might not get another chance.

'Mum?' she asked.

'Go,' said Margaret. 'I'll explain.'

'I can't just stop in the middle of the road,' the driver said as he pulled over to the side, tutting at her.

It only took another second or two but by the time he had stopped, the stranger had disappeared.

'Which way did he go?' Naomi asked, looking frantically from left to right as she held the door open, and stood half in and half out of the cab, scanning the crowds to the right and the crowds to the left.

'I didn't see,' said Margaret.

'Are you getting out or not?' The driver didn't sound happy. 'You're not the only one's who's running late.'

With his words ringing in her ears, Naomi took a final look around, before she settled back onto the seat.

'He's gone,' she said.

'Drive on please,' said Margaret, squeezing her daughter's hand.

'Make your mind up,' said the driver.

Margaret ignored him. 'You'll see him again, darling. At least you know he hasn't gone far.'

'And now we're stuck again,' the driver declared.

Thankfully, despite the traffic, Naomi and Margaret arrived at the Bridal shop as the clock on the town hall struck four, and Margaret smiled.

'It was a good thing you suggested we left early, darling.'

'Yes. I might not have seen the stranger if we'd left at any other time.'

Naomi pushed the door open and let her mum go in first.

'You're here!' Fiona could not contain her surprise. 'What's wrong? You look miserable.'

'I saw the handsome stranger but he was gone before I could stop him.'

Fiona glanced from Naomi to Margaret and back again.

'The one from the café? Where? In Betancourt Bay?'

'No.' Naomi shook her head. 'In Folkestone. Just a few minutes' from here.'

'Wow. So he's local then?'

'Or on holiday,' said Margaret.

'If he comes to Folkestone for his holidays, you're better off without him,' joked Fiona.

'He might be here on business,' Naomi said.

'He was wearing jeans,' said Margaret.

'People wear jeans at work,' Naomi pointed out.

'Only certain types of businesses let their staff wear jeans to work,' said Fiona. 'You'd be sacked if you wore them at my company. He probably works somewhere that allows him to be ultra trendy, ultra casual, or ultra scruffy. Or maybe he doesn't work at all. It is four in the afternoon and he's wandering the streets.'

'Crossing a road is hardly wandering,' Margaret said.

'We're wandering the streets and we work,' said Naomi

'I'm retired,' said Margaret.

'Hello,' said the shop assistant, who had been hovering in the background but who was now obviously keen to get on. 'Are we all here? Unfortunately the owner has been called away, so I'll be assisting you today.'

'Probably thought we'd be late and would have to rearrange again, so didn't bother coming in,' said Fiona, sarcastically.

'No! That wasn't it at all,' said the assistant, looking genuinely concerned.

'It's all right, dear,' Margaret said. 'The owner is a friend of mine. And my daughter is right. Connie did leave champagne for us though, didn't she?'

A look of relief spread across the assistant's face. 'She did. Yes. And she told me that if you did ever arrive I was to let you have anything you wanted. Oh! I mean ...

Erm.'

Fiona burst out laughing as did Naomi and Margaret.

'Don't worry,' said Margaret. 'We won't breathe a word. Join us in a glass of bubbly, dear. Now what is your name?'

Twelve

'I felt sorry for Justine when she let slip what Connie had told her,' Fiona said as she, Naomi and Margaret sat in the Pizza Palace restaurant an hour later.

'Connie would've laughed,' said Margaret. 'But some customers might've been annoyed.'

'I'm starving,' Naomi said. 'As you're paying, I'm ordering a lot.'

Fiona grinned. 'Fine. Just remember you've got a bridesmaid dress to fit into and today was the final fitting.'

'And I've got three whole weeks before the Big Day.'

'Yes. And if you keep eating those chocolates Greg's family sent, you'll need three whole dresses sewn together.'

Naomi stuck out her tongue. 'Right. Now I'm ordering even more.'

'Knock yourself out. Let's have more champagne shall we? I'm in the mood for bubbly tonight. And as we're all going to win millions on the Lottery, we'll be drinking it forever more.'

'We can't all win millions, darling.' Margaret grinned at Fiona. 'We'd all need the same numbers to do that.'

'Let's compare.' Fiona got out her purse and so did Margaret but Naomi reached into her coat pocket. 'You can't leave that in your pocket! You'll lose it.'

'I don't have a purse. It was stolen, remember?'

'Haven't you bought a new one?' Fiona frowned at her.

'I didn't have any money to put in one, so no. Not yet.'

'I've got a few spare purses. I'll call Greg and tell him to take one to the cottage when he joins Dad tonight for their TV football marathon.'

'Your dad is really looking forward to it,' Margaret said.

Fiona smirked and then looked at the three Lottery tickets. 'We've all got vastly different numbers. I can't recall the last time I bought one of these.'

'Same here,' said Naomi, taking hers back.

'Do you think your lucky coin will make you a millionairess? What would you do if it did? Would you still want Betancourt Bay

Café? Or would you buy a yacht and live a life of luxury on the high seas? I'd buy the yacht, but Greg will want to go on every luxury train journey on the planet.'

'That sounds like fun,' said Margaret. 'Your dad and I have always said that one day we'll go on the Venice-Simplon Orient Express.'

'I'll treat you both if I win,' said Naomi. 'And I'd buy the café outright, if Griff will sell it. Oooh. That reminds me. I haven't told you the latest.'

'About the café?' Fiona leant forward, an eager smile on her face.

Naomi nodded. 'Griff's been in touch with the Dunpoles. He told them that he'd heard a rumour they might like to surrender their lease of Betancourt Bay Café, or sell it on to someone. He said they seemed unsure at first and maybe even a little standoffish, but when he told them that the only reason he was getting in touch was because he knew someone who might be interested, they were delighted.'

'Wow. That's great news.'

'Yep. Derek apparently also said that they weren't as young as they were when they signed the lease, and that running a café is hard work, the cold winters make it more difficult, and business isn't what it once was. He told Griff that if the person was genuinely keen, they would be fools not to take the offer. On the understanding that it is for market value, as they need the money for their retirement. And this is the best bit. He told Griff they are considering moving to Spain. That means they must've worked things out.'

'Spain? So Doris will finally get her wish.'

Naomi nodded. 'And I might get mine if things go to plan. Griff said that the best idea might be for him to allow the Dunpoles to surrender their lease and for him to pay them a sum of money that's equal to what they'd get if they sold. It'll be quicker and cleaner because that way he can grant me a new lease for a term we both want, and one that won't keep me tied up for years. I can always extend it if I want and because we're friends, he'll make sure I get a good deal. And he will, I'm sure.'

'Yeah. Griff's a good guy. He always was. I'm so happy for you. It looks as if your luck has changed for the better.'

'Fingers crossed,' Naomi said.

'Give Mum that Lottery ticket to look after. I'll call Greg now about the purse.'

Naomi pulled the ticket from her coat pocket once again and handed it to Margaret.

'I'll put yours in this compartment, and ours in this one. And I'll let you have yours back the minute we get home.'

Naomi laughed. 'I trust you, Mum. Now can we please eat?'

Thirteen

Naomi fell asleep the moment her head touched her pillow. It had been a wonderful but busy day and the news about the Dunpoles had made her so excited, she was ready to explode.

And then she had seen her handsome stranger and her heart had almost burst.

But she had lost him again.

Grace had told her that Griff had spoken to a friend of his and they'd soon have some ideas of how to go about trying to find the handsome stranger. That had made her both nervous and excited in equal measure.

And it had also made her very aware of how much she owed, not just to Grace but to Griff. Especially to Griff. He had gone above and beyond and although he had done it for Grace, Naomi was the one who was benefitting.

She would have to find a way to repay them for all their help and kindness.

She dreamt again of her stranger and felt extremely tired when she woke up.

This afternoon she had a visit to the doctor to get her clean bill of health, so the bags beneath her eyes and the feeling of exhaustion was not what she wanted today.

She showered, dressed and went down to breakfast. Her parents were already seated at the table.

Yawning she joined them.

'Morning darling. Oh dear. Didn't you get any sleep? You look tired.'

'Thanks, Mum. I slept like a log. Perhaps too heavily, because I feel like a log. Or more like a tree trunk.'

'I'll make you a lovely breakfast.'

Margaret poured her a glass of orange juice, and James poured her a large mug of coffee.

'We didn't win millions,' Margaret said, as she made toast. 'We didn't win a thing.'

'That's a shame. I should've put that coin into my savings, but it was nice to dream about being a millionairess.'

'You didn't win anything either?' James asked.

'Oh. I thought you'd checked my ticket.'

'No. I gave you your ticket when we got home and you put it in that purse that Fiona asked Greg to bring round last night.'

'Oh yes. Sorry. I really am tired today.'

'There's been a lot going on,' said James.

'I've written the numbers on that pad on the table.' Margaret nodded to the pad near to where Naomi was sitting.

'Thanks. I'll check later. My new purse is upstairs. I think.'

She wouldn't have won a fortune so there was no rush, and she simply didn't have the energy to run upstairs right now.

'Don't forget,' said Margaret. 'I know it's unlikely but someone has to win.'

'I won't forget. I've got that doctor's appointment this afternoon. Can one of you give me a lift into Folkestone later, please?'

'I'll take you,' said James. 'I need to drop in the paperwork for your old car. You do still want to accept the offer for it don't you?'

'Absolutely. I think it's more than generous, especially as it'll cost a small fortune to repair.'

It was only a few hundred pounds but it was better than she had expected. She had thought they might even charge her to scrap it. She knew they had probably given her more as she was James' daughter and he was friends with the owner.

'Are we baking today?' Margaret asked.

'No. I'm meeting Grace to go over a few things ready for Monday. I hope I can wake myself up before then because I need to be at my best.'

'Perhaps you've got a cold coming on, darling. You know Grace wouldn't be cross if you had the day off to rest.'

'I know she wouldn't. But it's not a good start, is it? And as I said, I've got the appointment with the doctor today.'

'What time are you meeting Grace?' Margaret asked.

'Lunchtime.'

'Then why don't you go back to bed after breakfast? I'll make sure I wake you in plenty of time. You really don't look well, darling.'

Perhaps her mum was right? Bed was probably the best place for her the way she was feeling. But how had this come on so suddenly? She felt fine yesterday.

She tried to eat the delicious breakfast her mum had cooked, but each bite was harder to swallow than the last and now her eyes were streaming.

Wasn't this just her luck?

Taking a day off sick would not look good to Grace and the rest of the Eversleys, not to mention they would have to cancel the doctor's appointment, which would mean her start as an events planner would need to be delayed.

And Griff would have doubts too about her ability to run the café. If she became sick once she had a lease, she knew her parents would step in and cover for her, but would

Griff let her have a lease on that basis?

Just when it looked as if things were beginning to go right for her, this had to happen.

'I've got to go back to bed. I feel like death warmed over.'

'I'll bring you up a hot lemon drink,' Margaret said. 'And I really think you should phone Grace now and tell her how you feel. Better now than an hour or two before you're due to meet. Or I can call her for you.'

'Thanks. But I should do it. And you're right. I'll call her now.'

Grace was very understanding. 'Oh no. You poor thing. I think there's a nasty bug going around. Hope has come down with it too. Stay in bed and look after yourself. I'll cancel the doctor's appointment and we'll reschedule when you're feeling better.'

'I am so, so sorry, Grace. I haven't felt this bad since ... I can't remember when.'

'You don't need to apologise. It's not your fault. Now get plenty of sleep and feel better soon.'

Naomi must have slept but she didn't feel as though she had.

'I've brought you that hot lemon,' Margaret said, gently waking her and helping her to sit up. 'Fiona called and she's not feeling well either, so she's also in bed. She never takes time off work so she must be feeling dreadful. Oh, but she said she checked her ticket last night and she didn't win anything on the Lottery.'

'That's a shame. No luxury train journeys for Greg then. I forgot to check mine when I came back up, but I know I won't have won. My purse is there if you want to check.' She raised her arm a touch but it ached so she dropped it back down. It was taking enough energy to hold her cup of hot lemon. 'On the top of the chest of drawers.'

'Oh yes. I see it.'

Naomi sipped the refreshing drink and felt slightly better, but not enough to do anything that might require getting out of bed.

She had finished the drink when she realised Margaret was still standing in front of the chest of drawers. She looked like a statue.

'Oh no. Am I having hallucinations now?' She tried to focus. 'Mum? Are you there or am I imagining it?'

Margaret slowly raised her head. She had been staring at something clasped in her fingers.

'You … you've won.'

'What? Oh. The Lottery. What have I won? A free lucky dip?'

Margaret slowly shook her head. 'No. A bit more than that.'

She sounded like a mouse. No doubt Margaret had caught this awful virus thing as well.

'That's nice.'

'It's a bit more than nice, darling. You ... you've matched five numbers and the bonus ball. I remember the numbers. And although I don't recall the exact amount you've won, I do remember it was in the region of one million, two hundred and fifty thousand pounds! Oh. My. God! You've won. You've won! James! Come up here!'

Naomi had no idea what happened after that. She could remember the room spinning, her mum shrieking, her dad jumping up and down, and then everything went black.

When she opened her eyes again, her parents were at her bedside and their smiles were as wide as the Grand Canyon.

'We've called the number on the back of the Lottery ticket, darling,' Margaret said, 'and it is correct. You're now a millionairess. Or you will be. How does it feel?'

'I ... what? I'm dreaming, aren't I?'

'No. You're not,' said Margaret.

James beamed at her. 'You really have won. We can't believe it either. But it's true.'

'Oh bloody hell! I've won? Really? Have you told Fi?'

'Not yet. We thought you might want to

do that.'

'My head is spinning, Dad. I ... I can't even think let alone speak to someone on the phone. Not even Fi. Please call and tell her. Only put it on speaker so that I can hear what she says.'

Fiona was even more astonished that Naomi had been.

'You have got to be kidding me! Naomi never wins anything. The only luck she ever gets is bad luck. Oh wow. I'm so thrilled for you, Naomi. Now you can buy Betancourt Bay Café outright, assuming you still want to. This is the best news ever. I just wish I didn't feel so rough or I'd be with you all right now. In fact, I'm going to get Greg to bring me over. Is that okay with you?'

'Yes of course, darling,' Margaret said. 'We've got one sick person in the house. We may as well have two.'

'What happens now?' Fiona asked. 'I mean, how does Naomi get her money?'

'We have no idea,' said James. 'The Lottery people said they need the ticket holder to call them and then they will go through everything.'

'We did a search online,' said Margaret, 'and previous winners say that it only takes a few days until the money is in the winner's bank account.'

'The searches also revealed that once

Naomi calls the number on the ticket to confirm it's a winning ticket,' said James, 'the Lottery team will verify her identity and ask what bank account she wants the money paid into. They'll also check to see if there's anything she needs because it's such a huge shock to most people. Then, a couple of days later, one of the team will come here. They'll check through all the paperwork, ensure the ticket is real, and verify that Naomi is the person who bought it. That takes about an hour. Then the money can be sent to her bank account, or whatever account she wants, which will take about two days.'

'After that,' said Margaret, 'they can arrange meetings with legal and financial advisers. There's even a life coach. And a concierge service. If you want to travel on a luxury train, there are people who will organise it all for you. They can get you anything money can buy. Assuming you have enough to pay for what it is you want, of course.'

Fourteen

Everything happened exactly as James and Margaret had said it would. Except that, as Sunnycliff Cottage was not Naomi's registered address, the Lottery team had to verify that the flat in London was, and that Naomi had lived there until just a few days before. That didn't slow things down that much and the sum of one million two hundred and fifty-one thousand nine-hundred and forty-five pounds and thirty-two pence, was in Naomi's bank account in less than a week.

It was all so surreal.

She went to see Grace and Griff and explained everything in person. They were exceedingly happy for her, although Grace jokingly said she was disappointed that Naomi wouldn't be working for Eversley Events.

Griff was delighted Naomi was still interested in Betancourt Bay Café and when she said that rather than taking a lease on just the café, she would like to buy the property, including the flat that formed part of the premises, which the Dunpoles had used as a holiday let, and for storage, he said they could definitely do a deal.

'I want the café to be a place where everyone feels welcome,' she said. 'And I'll provide a hot drink or a meal for anyone who needs it. I want to have a special menu for those who are going through tough times and I'll call it The Lucky Coin menu. I haven't thought it all through yet but I don't want anyone to ever feel the way I did when I went into the café on that awful winter night. If it hadn't been for the handsome stranger, I still don't know what I would have done. I suppose I would have had to keep walking. No one should need to do that.'

'We'll get the ball rolling,' said Griff, 'and you'll soon be the owner of Betancourt Bay Café. Will you change the name?'

'No. I don't think so. After all, that night changed my life and the café was a part of that.'

'We'll have to have a proper celebration,' Grace said.

'We will,' said Naomi, 'and I'm going to pay for that.'

It was such a thrill for her to be able to treat people for a change. That was something she had not be able to afford to do for years. She had bought people small gifts and Christmas and Birthday presents, obviously, but to just treat someone to something simply because she could was a novel experience for her.

She would pay for all her family, including Greg of course, to travel on the Venice-Simplon Orient Express, because she knew her parents had dreamt of doing that, and obviously, so had Greg.

She would treat her friends in London to a holiday, or something that they really wanted. And she would donate to the charities she cared about.

There were so many things she wanted to do, and then a realisation hit her.

The amount of money she had won was way beyond her dreams. But once you had that sort of money, there were still lots of things that would be out of your reach.

One of the things the Lottery team advise people on is how to spend their winnings wisely and how to invest a certain amount to ensure a winner never runs out of funds.

People had won fortunes on the Lottery and were now bankrupt. That seemed almost impossible, and yet she could now see how easy it was to spend money if you had it.

She had never been extravagant and had

always tried not to get into debt and yet she had always worried about money.

Now she would never have to worry about it again. As long as she was sensible.

She had chosen not to have publicity. The last thing she ever wanted was to be famous. Not even for fifteen minutes.

Everyone in the village knew about her good fortune, but no one mentioned it unless she brought it up. Not even Barbra Brimble and that was a real surprise. That woman gossiped about everything. Naomi wondered whether Griff had had a word with Barbra. The woman idolised him and if he had told her not to mention it, it might tear her to pieces every day, but she would do as he asked.

Naomi's life was going to be so different now and she was excited about her future.

There was just one thing that was missing.

But money couldn't buy love.

It could however, buy a rearranged celebration dinner for her and Fiona's family, and for Greg's, and that was something Naomi wanted to do, especially as she had messed up the first one, albeit not entirely due to any fault of hers.

Fiona and Greg had decided it would be better to have it after the wedding, because there was so much happening already, but then someone had suggested to Fiona that the night before was a good idea.

'That's what they do in the USA,' Fiona said. 'And it means people coming to both the dinner and the wedding, don't have to travel to Betancourt Bay twice. Although they do have to travel to Folkestone and then up here to St Gabriel's Church for the wedding, and back down to Folkestone again for the reception and the disco. But they only need to be in the area for one weekend this way, not two. I don't know why we didn't think of it before.'

'Because it was my mum who organised the first celebratory dinner,' Greg had reminded her.

'Let me pay for this one,' Naomi had said, and Fiona and Greg, and Greg's mum, had gratefully agreed.

So now as well as buying a café and redecorating it, together with the flat on the property, Naomi was also going to have to help organise this dinner.

She needed some fresh air. It was Saturday evening, exactly two weeks after that night she had met the handsome stranger.

She walked towards Betancourt Bay Café, even though she didn't have the keys as yet, because the legalities were still being dealt with and Doris and Derek still held the lease.

She was surprised to see the lights were on and even more surprised to see two people seemingly arguing in the doorway. Were Doris and Derek at loggerheads again?

One of them was definitely Doris. Naomi could hear Doris' high-pitched voice wafting towards her on the chilly evening air.

'I've told you several times that I don't know,' she said. 'And even if I did I wouldn't tell you. My husband will be back any minute so you'd better go or there'll be trouble.'

'All I'm asking for is a name. Or a phone number.' The other voice was deeper, and softer.

'Go away. I'll call the police,' Doris shrieked.

The other person was also much taller and broader and...

No. It couldn't be.

Could it?

Naomi hurried towards the café as fast as her newly repaired boots would let her and then, as if he sensed her presence, the handsome stranger turned around.

'You're here?' she said, unable to think of anything else to say.

'Hello again,' the stranger said, his eyes dancing with delight and his voice as soft as a caress. 'I can't believe you're here. I've been thinking about you ever since that night. I hope that doesn't sound weird.'

'It does,' said Doris.

Naomi ignored Doris and beamed at him. 'It doesn't sound weird at all. It sounds wonderful.'

'It does? That's good because I can't seem to stop thinking about you. I dream about you every night. I even thought I'd seen you, down in Folkestone, once or twice. Is that too much? Please don't think I'm a stalker or anything because I'm not.'

'You sound like one,' said Doris. 'I'd run if I were you.'

Naomi tutted at her and smiled at the stranger. 'It's not too much. It's perfect. I dream of you. And I definitely did see you in Folkestone but you vanished into the crowds.'

'Erm,' he glanced at Doris and then smiled at Naomi. 'I know our favourite café is closed,' he rolled his eyes in jest, 'but would you like to go somewhere for a coffee? Or a hot chocolate? Or a glass of wine or something?'

'I'd love to. I know just the place. The Royal Oak pub. It's over there.' She pointed to the pub the lights of which cast a golden glow all around it.

'Perfect,' he said. 'Shall we?' He indicated with his hand that they should move towards it.

'If you get murdered this time, don't come running to me,' yelled Doris.

Naomi laughed but then threw him a sidelong glance. 'You're not going to murder me are you?'

'Not tonight.' He stopped in his tracks and actually blushed. 'I'm joking. Sorry. I'm not a murderer. I'm just an ordinary guy.'

'Phew. I had to ask. Only the universe and I have had some differences of opinion on what and what is not a helpful thing to send to someone who is asking for assistance.'

He furrowed his brows. 'I'm not sure I follow.'

'Don't worry. I'll explain over a drink.'

He smiled and as they walked on, he kept glancing at her. 'I know this sounds stupid but it took me a while to realise that I had your sister's phone number, because you used my phone to call her. Only when it eventually clicked, and I tried to call your sister this week, she must've thought I was a scammer or something and disconnected the call, and then blocked me.'

'She did what?' It hadn't occurred to Naomi, or to Fiona, obviously, that they had his number on Fiona's phone log all along.

'It's not her fault. I think I probably shouldn't have started the call with the words, "I've been looking for..." But that was as far as I got before she cut me off. And then after the second time she blocked my number.'

Naomi couldn't help but laugh. 'Fiona hates cold calls or any calls from unknown numbers. She gets a lot for some reason.'

'Please apologise to her for me. Or ... maybe I'll be able to apologise to her myself? Erm. I suppose I should've asked this first. Are you seeing anyone? And if you're not, would you consider, maybe, going on a date with me? I know it's fast and I know we've only met briefly, but the minute I saw you it was as if I'd known you all my life. Corny. But true.'

'Not corny at all. I felt the same. And no. I'm not seeing anyone. And yes. I would love to go on a date with you. Assuming you're single too.'

'Yes. I'm single. Or I was until now.'

They smiled at one another and then a thought popped into Naomi's head.

'Oh wait! There's a very important question I need to ask you first.'

'Ask away.'

'What is your name?'

They both laughed.

'That might help move things forward, I suppose,' he said. 'My name is Lucas. Lucas Dove. What's your name?'

'It's lovely to see you again, Lucas. I'm

Naomi. Naomi Hart.'

'Naomi Hart. That's a lovely name. You don't know how pleased I am to see you again, Naomi.'

'Actually, I think I do,' she said. 'And I also think I might owe the universe an apology.'

If her car had not broken down that night, along with her phone battery dying, she would not have been walking along London Road. And if she had not been walking along the road, she would not have crossed paths with the mugger. And if she had not been mugged, she wouldn't have gone to the café, she wouldn't have fainted, and gorgeous Lucas Dove wouldn't have caught her in his arms. He wouldn't have bought her a hot chocolate or let her use his phone. So they wouldn't have spent even one minute together, if not for all of that. And the idea of running the café would never have occurred to her because she wouldn't have known it might be available.

Sometimes, when you think the universe is sending bad stuff your way, it might be doing it for a very good reason. Or in this case, two very good reasons.

'I'm definitely thanking the universe for sending me to the café that night,' he said. 'I took the wrong road and got completely lost. I've recently moved to Folkestone and I haven't got my bearings. I stopped at the café because I thought it looked nice, and they might give me directions as my Sat Nav had clearly turned traitor. How wrong was I? But if I hadn't stopped there, I wouldn't have met you. And that is something I am very pleased about.'

As Lucas slipped his hand around hers she knew he felt the same surge of electricity that she had, and they smiled at one another as they walked hand in hand to the pub.

And to a bright and wonderful future together.

Just as the universe must have planned.

Coming soon

Visit www.emilyharvale.com to see what's coming next.

Plus, sign up for Emily's newsletter, or join her Facebook group, for all the latest news about her books.

Stay in touch with

Emily Harvale

If you want to be the first to hear Emily's news, find out about book releases, see covers and maybe chat with other fans, there are a few options for you:

Visit: www.emilyharvale.com

and subscribe to Emily's newsletter via the 'sign me up' box. Or, if you really love Emily's books, apply to join Emily's Open House here:

www.emilyharvale.com/MembersClub

Or ask to join Emily's exclusive Facebook Group here:

www.emilyharvale.com/FacebookGroup

Alternatively, just come and say 'Hello' on social media:

 @EmilyHarvaleWriter

 @EmilyHarvale

 @EmilyHarvale

A Note from Emily

Thank you for reading this book. I really hope it brought a smile to your face. If so, I'd love it if you'd leave a short review on Amazon, or even just a rating.
And, maybe, tell your friends, or mention it on social media.

A little piece of my heart goes into all my books. I can't wait to bring you more stories that I hope will capture your heart, mind and imagination, allowing you to escape into a world of romance in some enticingly beautiful settings.

To see my books, or to sign up for my newsletter, please visit my website. The link is on the previous page.

I love chatting to readers, so pop over to Facebook or Instagram and say, 'Hello'. Or better yet, there's my lovely Facebook group for the latest book news, chats and general book-related fun. Again, you'll find details on the previous page.

Also by Emily Harvale

The Golf Widows' Club
Sailing Solo
Carole Singer's Christmas
Christmas Wishes
A Slippery Slope
The Perfect Christmas Plan
Be Mine
It Takes Two
Bells and Bows on Mistletoe Row

Lizzie Marshall series:
Highland Fling – book 1
Lizzie Marshall's Wedding – book 2

Goldebury Bay series:
Ninety Days of Summer – book 1
Ninety Steps to Summerhill – book 2
Ninety Days to Christmas – book 3

Hideaway Down series:
A Christmas Hideaway – book 1
Catch A Falling Star – book 2
Walking on Sunshine – book 3
Dancing in the Rain – book 4

Hall's Cross series
Deck the Halls – book 1
The Starlight Ball – book 2

Michaelmas Bay series
Christmas Secrets in Snowflake Cove – book 1
Blame it on the Moonlight – book 2

Lily Pond Lane series
The Cottage on Lily Pond Lane – four-part serial
Part One – New beginnings
Part Two – Summer secrets
Part Three – Autumn leaves
Part Four – Trick or treat
Christmas on Lily Pond Lane
Return to Lily Pond Lane
A Wedding on Lily Pond Lane
Secret Wishes and Summer Kisses on Lily Pond Lane

Wyntersleap series
Christmas at Wynter House – Book 1
New Beginnings at Wynter House – Book 2
A Wedding at Wynter House – Book 3
Love is in the Air – spin off

Merriment Bay series
Coming Home to Merriment Bay – Book 1
(four-part serial)
Part One – A Reunion
Part Two – Sparks Fly
Part Three – Christmas
Part Four – Starry Skies
Chasing Moonbeams in Merriment Bay – Book 2
Wedding Bells in Merriment Bay – Book 3

Seahorse Harbour series
Summer at my Sister's – book 1
Christmas at Aunt Elsie's – book 2
Just for Christmas – book 3
Tasty Treats at Seahorse Bites Café – book 4
Dreams and Schemes at The Seahorse Inn – book 5
Weddings and Reunions in Seahorse Harbour – book 6

Clementine Cove series
Christmas at Clementine Cove – book 1
Broken Hearts and Fresh Starts at Cove Café – book 2

Friendships Blossom in Clementine Cove – book 3

Norman Landing series
Saving Christmas – book 1
A not so secret Winter Wedding – book 2
Sunsets and Surprises at Seascape Café – book 3
A Date at the end of The Pier – book 4

Locke Isle series
A Summer Escape – book 1
Christmas on Locke Isle – book 2

Betancourt Bay series
That Mistletoe Moment – book 1
That Winter Night – book 2

To see a complete list of my books, or to sign up for my newsletter, go to www.emilyharvale.com/books

There's also an exclusive Facebook group for fans of my books. www.emilyharvale.com/FacebookGroup

Or scan the QR code below to see all my books on Amazon.

Printed in Great Britain
by Amazon

37624103